S0-AFQ-393

Racing Against the Light

by Michele Spirn

AMSCO SCHOOL PUBLICATIONS, INC.
315 Hudson Street / New York, N.Y. 10013

Text Design by Merrill Haber

Cover Design by A Good Thing, Inc.

Compositor and Artwork: A Good Thing, Inc.

Please visit our Web site at:

www.amscopub.com

When ordering this book, please specify:
  either **R 695 P** *or*
  RACING AGAINST THE LIGHT

Amsco Originals

ISBN 1-56765-066-X
NYC Item 56765-066-9

PART

1

Chapter 1

The Voice on the Subway

Maybe you don't want to read this. I understand. I don't like to read much either, but I have to write this down. The last time I tried to tell somebody at the hospital, he didn't believe me. He tried to put me away. There are only two other people who know, and even they don't know everything. Somebody else has to know it all. It started with the light. I was standing in the first subway car. You can see the light as the train hits the track. It looks like the track is on fire. I like to watch it.

I was alone in the car. I had just finished work at the hospital. I work on the floors. I clean up and help the nurses. It's not the greatest, but the people are nice.

It was late but I wasn't scared to be on the subway. You hear that bad things happen a lot in New York. Some of it is true. Some of it isn't. But I think bad things can happen anyplace. You just have to know how to take care of yourself.

I was looking at the light when I started to feel funny. Not sick. Just strange. My head felt heavy. My eyes started to close.

I sat down.

I didn't feel bad, but I didn't feel like myself. The train stopped. Someone came into the car.

"Got a quarter?" a voice asked.

I looked up. It was a homeless man. They ride the subways a lot in New York.

"Just a quarter for a hot meal," he said.

I started to look for a quarter. I can't help it. I feel sorry for anybody who doesn't have a home. This man looked as if he really needed the hot meal. Then it started.

A voice inside me cried, "Why are you asking this boy for money? Even though you're half his size, you're twice his age. There's plenty of work at sea for men like you. Go down to the ships. Get a job! Stop bothering honest people!"

The homeless man looked around. There were only the two of us in the car. Where had the voice come from?

"What are you, a wise guy?" he asked.

"Never you mind," said the voice inside me again. "Get you gone. Now. Or else I'll call the law!"

"No need to do that. I'm going, I'm going." The train stopped at the Brooklyn Bridge station, and the homeless man ran off. I was as surprised as he was. What had happened? Where had the voice come from? Who was inside me?

I still felt strange, but now I was hungry. Very hungry. More hungry than I had ever been.

Seventh Avenue. My stop. I got off and

walked to the all-night pizza stand.

"Two slices," I said. "Plain."

I was happy to hear my own voice again. Maybe I had just been dreaming. Sometimes I fall asleep on the train.

I stared at the pizza sign while I waited. It lit up. Pizza. Big red letters. Then off. Then on again.

My slices came. I bit into one of them.

"Fah," the voice came back. "Bread and cheese. What kind of food is this for a man home from sea? Where's some red meat?" The pizza cook looked up.

"You okay?" he asked.

"And burned bread at that!" the voice cried.

"What's the matter? You don't like the pizza?" asked the cook.

"What did you put on it? It's all wet!"

"You asked for it plain," said the cook. "I got meatballs if you want."

"You'd never cook on Captain Billy's ship," cried the voice. "The men would throw you into the sea. Meat and potatoes. That's what we like. Captain Billy gives you plenty of it. No one goes hungry on his ship."

"Look, you don't like the pizza, you don't have to eat it," said the cook, glaring at me.

Everyone in the pizza place was looking at me. I could feel the voice starting again.

I turned and ran out the door.

"Meat!" cried the voice. "Red meat. Potatoes.

That's food fit for Captain Billy!"

"I give up," I thought. "I'll find a McDonald's."

It wasn't until I sat down with three quarter pounders and two large fries that the voice shut up.

I sat eating and thinking about what in the world was going on.

Was the voice Captain Billy? Where had it come from? How could I get it to stop? Most of all, if the voice ate like this every day, how was I going to pay for it?

Chapter 2

Get a Life

My place is three blocks from McDonald's. I walked home in the dark. I was afraid the voice would come back, but he was quiet.

Good. Maybe he would leave me alone.

I turned the key in the door.

"That you, Luke?" my mother called.

"Yep," I answered.

"Okay. Now I can go to sleep," she said.

My mother almost never goes to sleep until I come home. There's just the two of us—Mom and me. She works days and I work nights. So we don't see each other much. But we take care of each other.

"You're late tonight," she called from her bedroom.

"I stopped off for something to eat."

"I left supper for you. Put it away for tomorrow then," she said.

I turned on the light in the kitchen. Mom had also left some apple pie. I started to put it away.

"Not so fast."

Oh, no! Captain Billy, if that's who he was, had returned.

"Nothing like a good apple pie."

"Give me a break," I said. "You already ate like a horse.

Three quarter pounders. Two large fries. You'll make me sick."

"Have mercy, lad," said Captain Billy. "I haven't eaten in a very long time."

"How long?" I asked.

"About two hundred years," he answered.

"What?" I nearly fell off the kitchen chair.

"That's the last time I had a meal. I mean a real sit-down kind of meal," he said.

"Who are you? What are you doing here?" I asked.

"I came with the light," he said. "Now don't ask me any more questions. I want to enjoy this pie. I hope I'll be able to have more, but I don't know for sure."

"You have to answer me. What are you doing inside me?" I said. "I can't live like this."

"What's so bad about it?" asked Captain Billy. "We can work it out. You'll get to like me. Most people do."

"Turn off the TV, Luke," called my mother. "I can't sleep with all that noise."

"Okay, Mom," I called back.

"I don't want to get to like you," I said quietly. "Get a life."

"I have a life," said Captain Billy. "Yours. It's a good one. I'm very happy."

"We'll see about that," I said. I turned off the kitchen light.

I went to bed. I was dead tired. I'd deal with Captain Billy tomorrow, or maybe he'd disappear in the night.

The next morning I woke up late. My room was dark. We have windows on only two sides. The apartment is always dark. But I can tell what time it is by certain sounds and smells.

I could smell the coffee my mom had made. I could hear the bus as it stopped at the corner. I looked at my clock. Yep. It was 11 A.M. I'd better hurry if I wanted to make the game. I grabbed some orange juice. I threw on a pair of old shorts and ran down to the Y.

They were waiting for me. The sun tried to come through the windows. No one had turned on the lights yet. The Bear was trying free throws. Snake was watching. The rest of them were on the court.

"Ready?" I asked. We started the basketball game. I felt great. I was hitting all my shots. Then The Bear—all 210 pounds of him—sent me flying.

As I fell on the floor, I looked up. The Bear turned on the lights.

"Let's have some light," he said. "It's too dark in here to see."

"Why don't you turn the light on in your head?" Captain Billy was up and angry.

The Bear looked at me. I had never said anything like this to him before.

"Shhh!" I said to Captain Billy.

"Don't let people push you around. Stand up to him. Captain Billy never runs from a fight."

What was I going to do? Captain Billy was pushing me into a fight with the biggest guy I knew. The Bear looked angry.

"Shut up!" I said.

"Who you telling to shut up?" asked The Bear. No one had ever talked to him this way.

"Myself! I'm telling myself to shut up," I said. "What's a little push? It's all part of the game. Just like the food after the game. Sorry, Bear. I lost my head."

"Okay," said The Bear. "Let's play."

The Bear helped me up from the floor. I stopped to tie my shoe.

"Food?" asked Captain Billy quietly. "What kind of food?"

"You'll never know unless you shut up and let me play. Is it a deal?" I asked.

"I guess so," said Captain Billy. "But try not to get hit so hard, dear boy. It knocks the wind out of me."

"You can always leave if you don't like it," I said.

"Oh, no," said Captain Billy. "I'm not going anyplace."

"That's what I'm afraid of," I said. I went out to get in The Bear's way as much as I could. If

Captain Billy had the wind knocked out of him, maybe he'd stop talking.

And maybe I could think of a way to get him out of my life.

Captain Billy kept quiet after I had promised him food. When the game was over, I loaded him up with hot dogs and fries and cake.

"I never saw you eat so much," said the Bear. "You trying to catch up to me?"

"Just hungry today," I said. Except for a burp now and then, I heard nothing from Captain Billy.

Finally, I knew I couldn't eat any more. I paid and said good-bye to the guys. I had no place to be. But there was someone I wanted to see.

One of the bad things about working at night is there aren't many people around to hang out with during the day. Just when you're ready to have fun, they go to work. When you're working, they're having fun.

But there was one person I could visit while she was working.

It was my girlfriend Mariel.

She works at the library. I look at the books. At the same time, I try to talk to her. Sometimes it works. Sometimes she's too busy. But at least I get to see her.

Today was a good day. Ms. Burton, the head of the library, was upstairs. So we had a little time to talk.

"What are you doing today?" I asked.

"I have to update the computer," she said. "We've gotten some new books in. I have to list them."

"Do you think you could find out something for me?" I asked.

"What do you want to know?" she asked.

"I want you to find out about a man named Captain Billy," I said. "He lived in New York about two hundred years ago."

"Do you know anything else about him?" she asked.

"Only that he had a ship," I said. I felt something move inside me. I had done it. It was only a matter of time now.

Here it came.

"You son of a sea cook! You water rat! Getting a woman to do a man's job!"

"Luke!" cried Mariel. "What's the matter? You sound so strange!"

"You won't find out about Captain Billy as easy as that!" he stormed. "You'll be sorry you ever tried!"

Ms. Burton ran down the stairs.

"What's going on here?" she asked.

"It's okay," said Mariel. "Luke was just going." She pushed me to the door.

"I hope so," said Ms. Burton. "Don't let your friends come back again unless they can keep quiet. This is the library."

I hurried outside.

"See what you've done," I said. "Now you got Mariel in trouble. I hope she won't be mad at me."

"Serves you right if she is," said Captain Billy.

Chapter 3

TV or Not TV

By the time I left for work, Captain Billy had quieted down. We watched some TV together. It was all new to him.

"Tell me again, lad. This little picture comes on a box. You can see people doing things. And it's free?" he asked. He couldn't get over it.

At first, there was some trouble. I had turned on a movie about a ship caught in a storm. The captain made some bad moves. The men on the ship wanted to throw him into the sea.

"Fah! Not true! The captain was right. What do the men know?" he shouted.

"Let's watch something else," I said. I turned on "I Love Lucy."

He liked that. But he didn't get all the funny stuff. I tried to tell him what he missed. But he was about two hundred years behind. It was hard.

"Time to go to work," I said.

"Not yet," said Captain Billy. "Let's watch some more."

"I've got to go," I said. "I'll be late for work."

"One more show," he said. He was watching Hulk Hogan pick up a little guy and spin him around.

"No way," I said. I turned off the set. Not only was Captain Billy trouble, he was also becoming a couch potato.

He didn't say a word as I took the train to the hospital.

I guess he was still mad that he couldn't watch more TV.

I was cleaning the floor at the hospital when I ran into one of the nurses.

"Give me a hand, Luke," she said. "I need some help."

"Sure, Susan," I said. "What do you want me to do?"

"I need to bring this man into X ray. Push him into the room, and help me get him on the table. Then stay with him until they're ready to do the X ray. I have to go back to the ER."

I helped Susan and then waited. The man was asleep. He lay quietly under the X ray machine. I felt something inside.

"Is that what I think it is, lad?" came Captain Billy's voice.

"What do you mean?" I didn't understand what he was talking about.

"Let's just turn this on and see. I can't wait to find out what Lucy and Ethel are up to now." Before I knew it, Captain Billy had moved my hand. The X ray was on.

"What are you doing?" I yelled.

"Where are the pictures?" he asked. "Where's Lucy?"

"This isn't a TV. It's for taking pictures of the body," I said.

I turned the X ray off.

"You can't play with this like it's a toy. It's a very important machine," I said.

"Sorry, lad," he said.

I hoped Susan wouldn't find out the X ray had been on. But I had more to think about than that. Captain Billy had made me do something. He seemed to be getting stronger all the time. "Everything okay, Luke?" Susan was back.

"Sure," I said. "I guess I can go now." I wanted to leave in case she found out the X ray had been on.

"Thanks for the help."

I left the X ray room and ran back to my broom. I was never so happy to clean floors. Captain Billy was big trouble and getting even bigger. I had to get some help.

Then I thought of something.

On my break, I went to get something to eat. I sat down at the same table as Dr. Rogers. He was the head shrink and supposed to be the smartest guy in the hospital.

I was in luck. Dr. Rogers was alone. He was eating and reading at the same time.

Now, how to get him to see me?

"Could you pass the salt?" I asked.

He looked up at me.

"You need salt for coffee and a muffin?" he asked.

"Oh, I guess not. Really, I wanted to ask you something," I said. "You see, I have this friend."

"What about your friend?" he asked. He frowned at me, but at least he wasn't reading anymore.

"Sometimes voices that aren't his come out of him," I said. I really didn't know how to say it.

"He hears voices?" the doctor asked.

"I guess you could say that. It's one voice. The voice of an old sea captain," I said.

"It doesn't matter who it is," he said.

"It does to my friend," I said. "What do you think he should do?"

"Your friend is a sick boy. Hearing voices is a very bad sign. If I were to see him, I would give him some strong medicine. Maybe he should stay in the hospital for a while until he stops hearing voices," the doctor said.

"I see," I said.

He got up from the table. Then he looked hard at me.

"It's important that your friend see a doctor," he said. "Tell him to call me."

"I will," I said.

"By the way, if you work here and you need to be in the hospital, the cost is very low."

"Oh, it's not me," I said. "I really did ask for a friend of mine."

"Sure you did," he said. Then he got up from the table and walked away.

I started to shake. What had I done? The doctor had guessed there was no friend. Now he thought I was out of my mind. Was he right? Was I really going out of my head? Did I really need a doctor's help?

As I sat thinking about it, I could feel Captain Billy begin to laugh—somewhere not so deep inside me.

That night when I got home Mom was still up. She looked tired.

"Did you wait up for me?" I asked.

"No, I just couldn't sleep," she said. "Sometimes it happens. I get to thinking about your Dad. Even after all these years, it's hard to believe he's gone."

"If he had just left work a little later," I said. "Then that car wouldn't have hit him."

"That's a sad word—'if'," Mom said. "So many times I thought about it that way. Then I decided to stop. We can't do anything to change what's passed."

"But if that guy hadn't had so many drinks ..." I started to say.

"That's why I hope you won't ever drink when you drive," said Mom.

"Don't even think about it. With what I make, it's going to be a long time before I buy a car," I said.

"There are more important things in life. Like going back to school. Or learning a trade. You could be something, Luke. You can do more than clean floors in a hospital," said Mom.

"I'm just not ready yet, Mom," I said.

We've talked about this before. I guess she's right. But high school wasn't that easy for me. I just got through. I need a break before I go back to school. If I do.

"Don't let your life pass you by, Luke," she said. "You need to do something now before it gets too late. Don't be like me. I never finished college. I married your father instead, not that he wasn't wonderful. I like my job. But I always wanted to be a teacher, and I can never do that. You need college for that."

"I'll think about it," I said. "That's the best I can do for now."

"Well, I'm tired," she said. "I guess I'll go to bed."

I kissed her goodnight. She looked good. Maybe she didn't dress up, and she could use a haircut, but she was still pretty.

"I almost forgot. Mariel called you. She said she found something. You can call her tomorrow," Mom said.

I went to bed, too. I'd call Mariel in the morning. I hoped I would find out more about Captain Billy. But for now, he was quiet.

I fell into a deep sleep. But in the middle of the night, I woke up. Something was happening. I could hear someone moving around the room.

"Who's there?" I called.

There was no answer. I was really scared. I picked up the bat next to my bed. Then I turned on the light. All I saw was a shadow.

"What the . . ."

"Shh, lad, it's Captain Billy."

"What do you mean?" I jumped out of bed.

"Something happened with that TV box in the hospital," said Captain Billy.

"You mean the X-ray machine?" I asked.

"Whatever," he said. "It seems I'm coming out. Isn't it wonderful?"

Chapter 4

A Little Light Reading

First thing in the morning I called Mariel. I needed to know anything I could about Captain Billy. I was glad he was no longer inside me. But now he was getting stronger and stronger. I didn't know what to do with him.

"Hi, Mariel," I said. "What did you find out?"

"Meet me at the library and I'll show you. I have to be at work at ten today," she said.

"I'll be there," I said. I took a quick shower and got dressed. Then I ate breakfast standing up. Captain Billy didn't talk to me. But I did see a shadow in front of the TV. The TV was tuned to *Magnum P.I.* and it was loud. Captain Billy seemed to like reruns.

I raced to the library and stood outside. I wanted to catch Mariel before she went in.

When she saw me, she opened her eyes wide.

"I never saw you get to the library so early," she said.

"I'll tell you about it later," I said. "Let's go in."

She had to hang up her coat. Then she had to talk to Ms. Burton. I waited, walking back and forth in the reading room.

Finally, Mariel came into the room with a very old book.

"What's that?" I asked.

"It's a book about sea captains," she said. "I found it yesterday. You can take it out."

"Does it have anything about Captain Billy?" I asked.

"Oh, yes. It seems he was quite famous in his day," said Mariel.

"What do you mean?" I asked.

"I'm not going to tell you. You'll have to read it yourself," she said.

"Oh, come on," I said. "I don't have time."

"You have the whole day. You never even open a book. The most you read is the newspaper. And that's just the sports. It's time you read something and did something," she said. "You can't just spend the rest of your life at the hospital."

"Have you been talking to my mother?" I asked.

"We did talk a little bit on the phone last night, before you came home," said Mariel.

"If you knew how important this was, you'd tell me," I said.

"If it's that important, you'll read it yourself," said Mariel.

"I have to go to work. I'll see you tomorrow night, okay?"

"Sure," I said. "That's if it's all right to go to the movies. We could stay home and read books."

Mariel laughed. "You'd never read two days in a row. I know when to give up."

I had to laugh with her. She knew me too well.

"Okay," I said. "See you tomorrow night."

"I'll expect a book report on Captain Billy," she said as she walked off.

When I got home, something jumped on me. It wasn't heavy, but I could feel it. I shook it off.

"It worked for Magnum and Hulk Hogan," I heard Captain Billy say.

"What are you doing?" I barked.

"I tried a surprise attack," he said. "I saw it today."

"Captain Billy, you are really watching way too much TV."

"But you learn so much from it."

"I'll turn on the radio," I said.

"What's that?" he asked.

"Another special box," I said. I left him listening to "Talk Radio" while I went into the bedroom and locked the door.

After I read the first few pages, I was glad I had locked myself in. It was a terrible story.

First I read about the awful things some of the sea captains had done. They had killed people at the drop of a hat. They had taken slaves from Africa. Then they made them stay in the bottom of the ship without food or water for days on end.

When the ship got to America, the captains sold the Africans who hadn't died.

I had just gotten to the part about Captain Billy when I heard him.

"Can I come in, lad?" he asked.

"No," I said. "I'm busy."

"What are you doing?"

"Nothing you'd be interested in," I said.

"But Rush just told me something important," he said. "It's about all these new people coming to America. They're taking our jobs away."

"Not mine," I said. I was just getting to Captain Billy's story.

"It could be yours. It could be anybody's," he said. "Rush is very angry."

"You and Rush can cool it," I said.

"And I have another important message. They've found something new to get your clothes cleaner," he said. "It's a big break-through."

"My clothes are clean enough," I said.

Just then I heard a noise. I saw part of the Captain Billy shadow coming under the door.

Then he started to cry.

"I'm stuck! I'm stuck!"

I slid the book under the bed. Then I went over to help him.

As I opened the door, I said, "Too many Big Macs, Captain. You'd better start cutting down."

After that, Captain Billy stuck to me like butter to bread. I couldn't move without him.

I gave up trying to read the book. I didn't want him to know about it. I didn't think he had seen me hide it under the bed.

But when it came time for me to go to the hospital, he was willing to let me go alone.

I was just as glad. I was sick of Captain Billy. In the beginning, he had scared me. I didn't know where this voice was coming from. Then when I had gotten used to him as a voice, he came out. I started treating him like a pet. He was around, and he needed some taking care of.

But now he was getting brighter and stronger. He didn't seem like a shadow any more. If he went to the hospital with me, people might see him. And I really didn't know how to explain who he was.

I checked that the book was still under the bed. Then I left for work. Mom still hadn't come home. She was having dinner at her friend Lily's house.

I felt free as a bird. No Captain Billy. I could go to the hospital alone. I didn't have to be afraid that Captain Billy would do or say something. I felt just the way I had before Captain Billy had come into my life.

I made up my mind I'd have to do something about Captain Billy. I had to read that book. Maybe he'd be asleep tonight when I came home. Then I'd be able to read about him.

When I finished work, I still felt good. I stopped off for some pizza to bring home. I was very hungry.

I came into the house and saw that Mom was up again.

"Hi, dear," she said. "Your friend is waiting for you. He told me you said we could put him up. Of course I said 'yes'."

Captain Billy got up from the table. He was no longer a shadow. Now he was a man of about 40, dressed in old jeans and a striped shirt. For a minute or two, all I could do was stare at him.

"Captain Billy," I finally said. "How well you look."

"Never better," he said. "But call me Bill. My captain days are over."

"What do you do, Bill?" asked my mother.

"I used to work at sea. Now I'm thinking of getting into the hospital line. In fact, that's where I met your son," he said. "Hospital work would suit me just fine."

"I don't know if there are any jobs open," I said. "Seems like all these new people are taking them."

"So I hear," said Captain Billy. "But I'm sure you can find one for me. Can't you, lad?"

Mom made up a bed for Captain Billy in the living room.

"How long are you planning to stay with us?" she asked.

"Not long at all," I said. "In fact, Captain Billy has to be going very soon."

"Please call me Bill," he said. "How long I stay is up to you, Mrs. Mason. I'm sure I couldn't find a nicer place to stay, or nicer people to stay with."

"Let's move it, Captain," I said. "We're all tired."

Mom went to bed, and I got Captain Billy alone.

"What do you think you're doing?" I asked.

"She caught me in the hall," he said. "I had to say something to explain why I was there."

I grabbed him by the arm. I noticed he was much more solid now, even strong. Soon he would be stronger than I was.

"I want you out of here as soon as possible," I said.

"All right, boy," he said. He went off to bed.

Finally, we were all settled down. The house was quiet. Time to get on with my reading.

I reached under the bed. Good. The book was still there. I started to read, but I was having trouble keeping my eyes open. Try reading at two in the morning, and you'll see what I mean.

The next thing I knew I was asleep and in the middle of a terrible dream. I was tied to a bed. Men in white coats were standing over me.

One of them was Dr. Rogers.

"He looks all right," he said, "but he keeps hearing voices."

"I think we'd better give him something," said another.

"Maybe we should just let him rest until he's better," said Dr. Rogers.

"Without food and water," said Captain Billy.

"You're right, Captain," said Dr. Rogers. Everyone laughed.

I woke up with a start. I washed my face and felt better. I turned on my light. As long as I was up, I would read about Captain Billy.

I had almost finished Part Three about the sea captains who sold the Africans. It ended this way:

"There were sea captains who did other terrible things. One of the worst was Captain Billy Hawkins of New York, known as the Killer Captain."

I turned the page. But all I saw was the heading "Part Five. "All of the pages about Captain Billy had been neatly cut out. How was I going to find out about him? And how was I going to tell Mariel that her library book was missing some important pages?

Chapter 5

Captain Billy Makes a Move

The next morning Mom went all out for breakfast. Neither one of us worked on Saturdays, so she always made a nice breakfast for us. This time she outdid herself. There were eggs and pancakes and fruit and juice.

I just picked at my food, but Captain Billy chowed down as if he were storing it up for another two hundred years.

"This is first rate, Mrs. Mason," he said, in between bites.

"It's nice to feed a man again," my mother said.

"By the way, Bill, I'm missing part of a book I was reading," I said. "Did you see it?"

"Can't say I did," he said, looking straight at me. "What was it about?"

"Sea captains," I said.

"I don't know where the pages are," he said. "Of course, if there's anything you want to know, you can always ask me."

"How did you know there were pages missing?" I asked.

"Pages are part of a book," he said. "You said part of the book was missing."

He got up from the table and bowed to my mother. "That was wonderful, Mrs. Mason," he said. "I haven't had a meal like that in a long time. I have a little business to take care of. But I'll come back later. Maybe you'd like to eat dinner out with me tonight."

"That would be nice," said my mother.

"The honor is mine," he said.

I found my mother in the kitchen cleaning up.

"I like your friend a lot, Luke," she said to me.

"Mom, about Captain Billy," I started to say.

"You know, Luke, he's a lot like your father," she said.

"He's nothing like Dad," I said. "Dad was a great guy."

"I thought this man was your friend," she said. "I don't understand."

"He's not my friend at all," I said. "And I don't want you to go out with him."

"It's only dinner," Mom said. "I haven't had a man take me out to dinner in a long time."

"Please don't," I said.

"Why not?" asked Mom. "What's wrong?"

How could I tell her? What could I say? "Mom, I was riding the train one night when Captain Billy came into my life. He's some strange guy that lived two hundred years ago. Captain Billy is a ghost." I couldn't find the words.

Mom put her arm around me. "I'll never forget your father," she said. "I just want to have a little fun."

"Okay," I said. "But please, please be careful."

Mom went out to get her hair done. No one was in the house. So I looked all over for the missing pages. I found nothing, nada, zip.

It was getting late, so I ran to meet Mariel at the movie. The picture was great, but I couldn't keep my mind on it. I kept thinking about Captain Billy and Mom. After the movie, Mariel and I went out for pizza.

"I'm ready for your book report," she said, laughing.

"Something happened," I said. "I'll tell you about it later. I didn't get the chance to read about Captain Billy. But it's very important. Please tell me what you found out."

"I should have known you wouldn't read it," she said. "Okay, here's the story. Two hundred years ago Captain Billy and his men were coming into New York on the ship Good Hope. They were an hour away. The captain gave one of the men an order to do something. The man didn't do it. So the captain got a gun. He held it to the man's head and made him jump off the ship. The man died in the ocean."

"Didn't any of the other men tell on him?" I asked.

"He said he would kill any of them who did," Mariel said.

"So how did anybody find out about it?" I asked.

"Soon after, Captain Billy was killed in a fight in a bar. One of the men wrote home about it. Soon everybody knew. But it was too late to do anything about it."

"What a story!" I said. "It's hard to believe Captain Billy was such a cold killer."

"So how come you didn't read the book?" asked Mariel.

"I did read part of it," I said. I didn't know how to tell her the rest.

"Luke, I know you're not telling me something," she said.

"I don't know how to tell you this," I said. "But the book isn't the way you gave it to me."

"What's wrong with it?" she asked.

"Some of the pages are missing," I said very quietly.

"What?"

"Some of the pages are missing."

"That does it!" Mariel jumped up from the table. "That's a library book. We don't have another like it. Now I'll have to tell Ms. Burton what happened. She'll be angry with me. I'll have to listen to her all day. And I didn't even do anything."

"I'm really sorry," I said. "I didn't do it."

"Oh, Luke," she said. "Who *did* do it? Captain Billy?"

"As a matter of fact, yes," I said.

"Can't you do any better than that? If you really cared about me, this wouldn't have happened.

I've had it. Call me when you grow up." And Mariel stormed out of the pizza place.

Dr. Rogers thought I was out of my mind. Mom thought I was wrong about Captain Billy. Mariel thought I didn't care about her. I never felt so alone in my life.

I didn't hear Mom and Captain Billy come home that night. But I saw Mom's face the next day. She looked really happy.

"Oh, Luke," she said. "I haven't had such a nice time since your father died."

"What did you do?" I asked.

"We went out to dinner to that new seafood place," she said.

"Then we went dancing. I haven't danced in so long. It was like a dream."

"I see. Where's Captain Billy now?" I said.

"Right here, lad," he said, coming into the kitchen.

"Sit down, Bill," said my mother. "I'm just making the coffee."

"Thanks, Mary," he said. "I just want to take a look at the want ads. I need a job."

"Luke, weren't you going to help Bill find something at the hospital?" she asked.

"I'm sure Bill doesn't want to work in a hospital with all those sick and dead people," I said. "It's not a happy place."

"I'll take anything I can get," said Captain Billy. "The problem is it's not so easy at my age to get something."

"You look young to me," said my mother. "But Luke will help you look for a job tomorrow, won't you?"

"If I have to," I said. I didn't want to make this easy.

Then I had a thought. "I guess you'll be moving out soon once you get a job."

Captain Billy looked down at the floor.

"Of course," he said. "I don't want to make more work for you, Mary."

"It's no work at all," said Mom. "I wouldn't hear of you moving right now. Once you've saved some money, then you can think of it."

"If I get a job, how about if I give you some rent?" asked Captain Billy. "I wouldn't feel right if I didn't."

"I can't say it wouldn't be a help," said Mom. "Right, Luke?"

I just looked at both of them.

"Then that's settled," said Captain Billy. He threw the newspaper on the table and went to get a cup of coffee.

I couldn't move. All of this was going way too fast for me.

But The Bear and Snake were waiting for me. Time to play. I felt so mean all I could do was hit people. I certainly wasn't hitting any baskets.

After half an hour, The Bear caught on.

"What's wrong with you, man?" he asked.

"Nothing," I said.

"Doesn't look like nothing to me. Come on," he said.

"My girl and I had a fight," I said.

"That's nothing new," said Snake. "The Bear and his girl fight every week."

"You just wish you had a girl to fight with," said The Bear to Snake.

"That's not all," I said. I didn't know how to tell them about Captain Billy and my mom.

"What else?" asked The Bear.

"My mom's going out with a guy. I don't like him. He's moved in." That was the best way to put it.

"Uh, oh," said Snake. "That happened at my house. My mom took up with this guy. I knew he was a loser. He turned out to be a real rat. Ran off with her money and everything."

"What did you do?" I asked.

"What could I do?" Snake said. "Nothing. Now she's a lot more careful."

"The thing is, it's your Mom's life," said The Bear. "If the guy's no good, she's going to have to find out for herself. You can't do it for her."

"But this guy is really bad," I said. "I know him."

"You could move out," said Snake. "That's what I did when I couldn't stand it any more."

"I could never leave her alone with him," I said.

"Then you're going to have to put up with it," said The Bear.

"Now come on, let's play. I got to be out of here soon."

Chapter 6

Quiet in the Library

The next day I decided the only thing I could do was make up with Mariel. So I took the book and walked to the library.

I saw Mariel talking to Ms. Burton.

I went over to Ms. Burton and stood in front of her.

"Ms. Burton, I am very, very sorry," I said. "My little cousin Tommy was at my house. I didn't know he was playing with this book until it was too late. Some of the pages are missing. I tried to put them back. I couldn't. I will be happy to pay for the book. I am very sorry. It won't happen again."

Ms. Burton stood there with her mouth open. She looked at the book and then at me.

"Thank you for telling me about this. Most people who've done something to a library book try to hide it," she said. "I'll let Mariel know how much the book costs. I'm sure we can work something out."

She walked off and Mariel turned to me.

"Thanks, Luke," she said. "I was just about to tell her when you came in. You saved me a lot of trouble."

"I am sorry," I said. "You were right."

"But what really happened? You don't have a cousin Tommy," she said.

"I have to tell you," I said. "If I don't tell someone, I'll go nuts."

"What is it?"

I didn't know how to say it. I thought about it for a minute.

"Did anything strange ever happen to you?" I asked.

"One time I had a dream about money. The next day my Mom won $50 in the Lotto. Is that the kind of thing you mean?"

"It's a little more strange than that," I said. "Did you ever hear of anyone coming back to life?"

"You're scaring me, Luke," she said. "What are you talking about?"

"It's Captain Billy. He's come back," I said. "I think he's the one who took those pages."

"What?" cried Mariel.

"Shhh!" said Ms. Burton. "Please. We need to be quiet in the library."

It was the wrong time to tell Mariel about Captain Billy. She was in the middle of work. She was working until eight that night. I was supposed to be at the hospital then.

"How about if I meet you tomorrow afternoon?" I said.

"You bet," said Mariel. "I don't have to work tomorrow. And I can't wait to hear your story."

She seemed to be taking it well. I felt better.

"I'll meet you at the Promenade," I said. "We can walk and talk."

"Okay," she said. "I'll see you there at two."

Then she looked at me. "You are all right, aren't you, Luke?"

"Of course I am," I said. "Please don't think I'm nuts. Just wait until you hear my story."

"I can't wait," she said. Then she turned back to where Ms. Burton was waiting for her with a pile of books.

As for me, I got a hot dog and an orange drink from a cart on the street. Then I sat down on the library steps to think.

What was I going to do about Captain Billy? I had to take him to the hospital. Mom would make sure of that. What could I do to get him out of our lives? How could I make it hard for him to be around us?

Captain Billy was mean enough to watch a man die. He was tricky, too. Look at how fast he got Mom to take him in and to like him. He seemed to be ten steps ahead of me all the time.

How could I get him to go? I leaned back against the steps and slowly sipped my orange drink. I looked at the people going in and out of the courthouse across the street.

The courthouse! Of course. That gave me an idea. I could talk about it with Mariel. I felt a lot

38

better. Maybe Captain Billy didn't hold all the cards. Maybe I could beat him at his own game. Maybe he didn't know so much after all.

I went home to catch up on some sleep. With one thing and another, I hadn't gotten much rest.

Before I even had a chance to dream, Mom was waking me up.

"Time to get up, Luke. Bill is waiting for you to help him find a job. He's found an ad that wants men to do heavy work on a building."

I got dressed. There he was sitting in the living room waiting for me. I was angry. Captain Billy had moved in to my house. My mom liked him. Now he was cutting into my sleep time.

"Good luck," said Mom, as we left the house.

As we walked to the train, I thought how tired I was of Captain Billy and doing things for him. Time to have a little fun, my way.

"You know, Bill," I said, "you really should get some new clothes before you ask for a job."

"What's wrong with what I've got on?" he asked.

"It's not good to go looking for a job in jeans," I said.

"But that's what you're wearing," he said.

"But I have a job," I said. "I can wear what I want. You, on the other hand, need to get more dressed up."

"Maybe you're right," he said. "But I don't have much money. That's why I need the job."

"I thought all you sea captains had lots of gold," I said.

"I do," said Captain Billy. "But I'd have to go back to get it."

"Maybe that's something you should think about," I said.

"Oh, no," said Captain Billy. "I like it here just fine."

"Here's a good place to get some clothes," I said. "Tell you what. I'll even loan you some money."

"That's very kind of you, lad," he said.

A man in the store came up to us.

"May I help you?"

"We'd like to see something for him," I said.

"Certainly. We have lots of things for your father," he said.

"He's not my father," I said.

"Who knows, lad," said Captain Billy. "Your mother certainly has made a play for me."

I had started to feel bad about playing this trick on Captain Billy. Now I didn't care anymore.

"Let's see what you've got," I said to the man.

When Captain Billy and I came out of the store, people looked at him.

"It's wonderful you don't have to buy these clothes. You can just rent them," he said. Then he saw people looking at him.

"What are they looking at?" he asked.

"You look so good in your new clothes," I said.

"In my day, nobody looked at you like that," he said.

"It's two hundred years later," I said. "Keep up with the times."

We got to the building. Some of the guys were on break outside. They started whistling.

"Who's the dude?" asked one guy.

"Where you going?" asked another. "To the MTV awards?"

They all started laughing.

Captain Billy was angry. He turned to me.

"What's wrong with these clothes?" he asked. "Aren't they good enough to get a job?"

"A job!" The guys laughed and laughed.

"Yeah," said one of them. "A job! Sure! If you want to wait on tables."

Captain Billy looked down at his white tie and tails.

"You mean these clothes aren't right?" he asked. "I thought I was just behind the times."

"Don't pay any attention to them, Captain," I said. "They just like to laugh at everybody."

"I don't think so," he said. "You tried to trick me. And if you think I'm going to pay you back, forget it."

"It was worth every penny," I said. "Don't ever talk about my mother like that again."

"And what do you think she'll say when I tell her what you did?" asked Captain Billy. And he turned and walked back to the subway.

Chapter 7

He's a Stranger

Of course, Mom was waiting up for me when I got home. Of course, Captain Billy was hiding in the bathroom.

Mom was ready for battle.

"How could you do that to Bill?" she asked. "To make fun of him like that. He's a stranger here. We have to help him. We should be kind to him."

"Mom, don't you think it's strange he doesn't know how to dress?" I asked.

"Of course not. He's been on a ship all those years. He doesn't know about getting a job on land."

"Oh, sure," I said. I could see this wasn't the time to tell her the real story of Captain Billy.

"I feel terrible, Luke," she said. "I thought I raised you better than this."

Then Captain Billy stepped out of the bathroom.

"Now don't blame yourself, Mary," he said. "You did the best you could. After all, the boy doesn't have a father."

That did it.

"I did have a father," I said. "And he was ten times the man you are."

"Luke," said my mother. "Please say you're sorry to Bill."

"I won't," I said. "And if Bill knows what's good for him, he'll go back where he came from."

"Maybe I should go, Mary," said Captain Billy. "It hurts me so to see you two fighting."

"I won't hear of it, Bill," said my mother. "And I want to pay you back for the money you spent on those clothes."

"Please don't, Mary," said Captain Billy. "I won't spend any more money for the next two weeks. Then maybe I'll be able to buy some other clothes."

"What?" I shouted. "He didn't spend a penny on those clothes. I did."

Captain Billy just looked at me sadly.

"How can you tell such lies?" I asked.

"Never mind, Luke," said my mother. "It's settled."

Captain Billy was really taking over my life. And not only that. My family was using all its money to put clothes on his back.

The next morning I didn't see Mom. Captain Billy was up and watching an old Elvis movie. He seemed really interested. We didn't talk to each other. I had stayed away from Mom and Captain Billy the night before. You might say I had closed the door hard after Mom told me everything was settled.

It was hard to take. My own mother didn't believe me. That really hurt. I didn't understand what was happening. Captain Billy had turned my world upside down.

Now I was on my way to tell my girlfriend that a sea captain from two hundred years ago had taken over my life. She probably wouldn't believe me either.

I had picked the nicest place I knew to tell her my story. From the Promenade, you can look across the East River and forget you'd never even want to stick a finger in it. It looks so clear and shiny. There are big ships and little boats on the water. They're all going someplace in a hurry. And above it all is the skyline of New York. The tall buildings look so close you could touch them.

Mariel and I sat down on a bench.

"So what's up?" she asked.

I told her the story. My heart was in my mouth. Would she believe me?

"It's so strange," she said. "I don't know what to think. Are you sure somebody isn't playing a trick on you?"

"I'm sure," I said. "This guy doesn't even know who Elvis is."

"But still it's so hard to believe," she said.

"Look, you can believe it or not, but why would I make this up?" I said.

That got her. She looked like she was thinking hard.

"I guess there's no reason for you to make it

44

up. What are you going to do?" she asked.

"I have to find a lawyer," I said.

"My uncle's a lawyer," said Mariel. "We could go see him."

"Can you call and fix it up?" I asked.

"Sure," she said. "What do you want to see him about?"

When I told her, I wasn't sure she thought it was a good idea.

"It's worth a try," I said.

"Okay, I'll call him and set it up," she said. "But I hope he doesn't get mad."

"Your uncle or Captain Billy?" I asked.

"Both, I guess," she said.

I thought I'd get a little peace when I went to work that night. No such luck.

"There's a new guy," said Jim, the head cleaner. "He's here to help us."

"Hello, Luke," said Captain Billy.

"Oh, you know each other," said Jim. "That's good. I'll put you down to work together."

First my body. Then my house. Then my mother. Now my job.

I was sick of Captain Billy.

I grabbed my broom and walked off. Captain Billy followed me.

"Jim said you're supposed to show me what to do," he said.

"Never mind what Jim said. Get out of here," I said.

"Now, you know I'm not going to do that. I

45

need a job."

"But why my job?" I asked.

Captain Billy laughed. "Boy, you know what's yours is mine. Your body. Your house. Your job. And just maybe . . . your mother."

I turned my back on him.

"Just wait," I said, pushing my broom. "I'm going to get even with you if it's the last thing I do."

I guess I was talking kind of loudly. I was so angry. Then I saw Dr. Rogers. He was looking at me strangely.

I turned around. Captain Billy was gone. I was all alone.

I tried to make the best of it.

"Hi, Dr. Rogers," I said.

"Hello," he said to me. "What's your name again?"

"His name's Luke," said Captain Billy. All of a sudden, he had come back.

"Well, Luke," said Dr. Rogers. "How long has it been since you've had a checkup?"

I told Dr. Rogers I had just had a checkup.

"But maybe he needs another one," said Captain Billy. "After all, he looks like he needs a rest. Doesn't he, Doc?"

"I don't need a rest. I'm fine," I said. "And you can mind your own business."

"You're lucky to have a friend who cares about you," said Dr. Rogers.

"I'm really okay," I said. "I have to get on with my work."

"Always working," said Captain Billy. "I'd like to see him get a nice rest. Don't you think so, doctor?"

"Hard work never hurt anybody," said Dr. Rogers. "Well, young man, if you find you're not feeling so well, let me know."

"I'll watch him," said Captain Billy. "I'll keep an eye on him."

As the doctor walked off, I poked Captain Billy with the broom.

"Just leave me alone," I said. "How did you get this job, by the way?"

"Your mother helped me," he said. "She felt so sorry for me after what you did. It was easy. Like taking candy from a baby. She took me down here. I met everybody. I got the job."

"Can't you leave her alone?" I asked.

"I like your mother," he said. "And she seems to like me. In fact, we're going out tomorrow night."

"Why don't you date someone your own age?" I asked.

"What do you mean?"

"Oh, somebody about two hundred years old," I said.

"Since I met your mother, I feel young," he said. "In fact, I feel more and more like your age."

"If you want to live to be three hundred," I said, "you'd better stay away from her."

"I'm not scared," he said. "You'd never be able to do anything to me."

"Don't be so sure," I said. "I'm working on it."

47

Chapter 8

Elvis Is Dead

Captain Billy was still watching Elvis the next morning. I guess it was Elvis Week on TV. He was even starting to sing some of the Elvis songs. Captain Billy couldn't sing his way out of a paper bag.

I played a fast game with The Bear and Snake. Then I washed and changed to meet Mariel at her uncle's.

He had an office on Court Street. He was thin and tall with dark hair and dark eyes. He looked a lot like Mariel.

"Uncle Hector, this is my boyfriend, Luke," said Mariel.

"Nice to meet you. How can I help you?" he asked.

"If someone killed someone, he can be put on trial, right?" I asked.

"He can be put on trial. Then we try to find out if he did it or not," he said.

"But what if someone killed a man two hundred years ago?" I asked.

"What kind of question is that?" he asked.

"I need to know," I said.

"I'm very busy," he said. "I thought you needed help."

Mariel's uncle was getting mad. She tried to make things better.

"Oh, Uncle Hector, this is for a class Luke is taking," she said. "He needs it for school."

"Oh, I see. Well, I'd have to look it up. But I think you can try someone at any time for murder," he said.

"Even if it's two hundred years later?" I asked.

"Even if it's two thousand years later," he said.

"Thanks. Thanks a lot," I said.

"Any time," he said. "What school do you go to?"

I didn't know what to say.

"New York College," said Mariel.

"Good luck," said her uncle.

We walked outside.

"Why did you tell your uncle I was going to school?" I asked.

"I didn't know what else to say," she said, looking away. Besides, what's so bad about being in school?" she asked, now looking down at her feet.

"Nothing. But I'm not," I said.

"But I wish you were," she said, looking at me.

Everyone was pushing me. First, my mom. Then Mariel. I should do something. I should make something of myself. Maybe they were right, but I wasn't going to tell them—yet. First, I had to take care of Captain Billy.

Meanwhile, Mariel was still looking at me.

"You're not mad at me, Luke, are you?" she asked.

"No, but I've got to take care of some business with Captain Billy," I said. "You want to come with me?"

"Sure, I'd love to meet him," said Mariel.

We found Captain Billy parked in front of the TV set. The only thing that showed he'd moved since I left was a dirty dish and glass.

"Captain, this is my girlfriend, Mariel," I said.

"How did a nice girl like you get hooked up with a boy like Luke?" the captain asked.

"Never mind," I said. "Let's talk business."

Captain Billy turned off Elvis.

"What's on your mind?" he asked.

"Captain, I know all about the killing," I said.

"What are you talking about?" he asked.

"That man you killed two hundred years ago because he didn't do what you wanted on the ship," I said.

"Have you lost your mind, boy? I don't understand you," he said.

"Come on, Captain Billy. You told the men on the ship to keep quiet. But one of them wrote a letter home and told on you," I said.

"Your boyfriend is really sick," said Captain Billy, talking to Mariel. "He thinks I'm someone named Captain Billy. He thinks I'm two hundred years old. We have to help him."

Mariel looked at me as if she weren't sure about me.

"He's trying to fool you, Mariel," I said. "Please believe me."

"Mariel, you want Luke to get well, don't you?" he asked. "Let me take care of him."

"I don't know what to think," said Mariel.

Then I had an idea.

"Captain, if you're not two hundred years old, prove it," I said. "Tell us what Elvis's latest hit song is."

Captain Billy thought for a minute.

"I don't really know. I've been very busy with my new job. But I'm sure it's as good as his last one, "Jailhouse Rock.""

"Gotcha, Captain," I said. "Elvis is dead."

"Oh no, boy, you're wrong. I just saw him on TV," said Captain Billy. "He can't possibly be dead."

"You really are two hundred years old," said Mariel. "You're a ghost. I'm looking at a ghost!"

Her eyes opened very wide. Then she stepped back, away from Captain Billy. She swayed as if she were about to faint.

"Now look what you've done," said Captain Billy to me.

It was a couple of minutes before Mariel could speak again. She could hardly look at Captain

Billy. She couldn't believe she was in the same room as a ghost.

"You were right all along, Luke," she said. "And to think I really didn't believe you. I was just going along with you."

Captain Billy kept looking at her as if he were trying to make her believe that he was a real person again.

I was happy. Finally, somebody besides me knew what Captain Billy was.

"You see, Captain, you're going to have to leave now," I said.

"There are two of us who know about you."

"Not so fast," he said.

"You don't really think you can still stay?" I asked.

"And why not?" he asked. "You can't tell your mother about me. Look what it did to your girlfriend. She nearly fainted. And she doesn't even know me. It could kill your mother."

I hated to admit he was right.

"But Captain, I talked to a lawyer today," I said. "You can still be tried for killing that man."

"Who cares? His family is all dead by now. There's no one who's interested in something that happened two hundred years ago," he said, laughing.

"There must be somebody interested," I said.

"Who will believe you?" he said. "Everyone will think you're out of your mind. Just like that doctor at the hospital."

"What doctor?" asked Mariel.

"Dr. Rogers. He thinks there's something wrong with me," I said.

"I told him I would keep an eye on you," said Captain Billy. "It would be easy for me to tell him I thought there was something wrong. You could have a nice long rest in that hospital if I were to open my mouth."

"You wouldn't do something like that, would you?" asked Mariel.

"Of course," said Captain Billy. "So if you don't want your boyfriend shut up with the psychos, you'll keep quiet about me."

"I'll get you somehow," I said.

"Just remember, all I need to do is talk to Dr. Rogers and you'll be put away for a long time," said Captain Billy. "Not as long as two hundred years, but long enough."

By the time we left, Mariel was mad.

"Who does that Captain Billy think he is?" she said. "I have the whole library at my fingertips. I'll find a way to make him go away."

For the next two days she looked up everything she could on magic and spells. She found books that told about dreams. She found ways to use black cats in magic. She found out how to make rabbits come out of a hat. She found out the secrets of witches. But she couldn't find anything to make ghosts go away.

"Ms. Burton is starting to wonder what I'm doing," she said to me. "I have to stop. But I'll keep on thinking."

As for me, I tried to be as mean to Captain Billy as I could. Maybe then he would go away.

At home, I put lots of pepper in his food when Mom wasn't looking. But he ate up anyway.

I hid the TV Guide from him. But he didn't care. He just channel-surfed. Then I turned down the sound and told him the TV was broken.

But when he told Mom, she fixed it.

At work, I couldn't do much. There were too many people around.

And from time to time, Captain Billy would look at me when Dr. Rogers passed by.

I was just thinking I would have to get used to Captain Billy or leave home, when Mariel called.

"Meet me outside the library," she said. "I have an idea."

I ran all the way. I could hardly wait.

"What is it?" I panted.

"We thought of making Captain Billy go away," she said. "But we couldn't find anything."

"Right," I said. "So?"

"So how about bringing out another ghost?"

"What do you mean?" I asked.

"There were other men on that ship. Wouldn't they be angry with Captain Billy for killing their friend?" she asked.

"I guess so," I said.

"Maybe one of them would fight Captain Billy," she said.

"At least he might chase Captain Billy away."

"Sounds like a good idea," I said. "How would I get someone like that?"

"The same way you got Captain Billy," she said. "Just stand in the first subway car again and look at the light."

Chapter 9

Return to the Light

I had a big fight with Mariel.

"I won't do it," I said. "I can't believe you want me to. It was terrible. I couldn't stand it again."

"I wish I could think of something else," she said. "But I can't. And the way things are going, Captain Billy will never leave."

I didn't want to listen to her. I went home mad. I thought about it all night. When I did fall asleep, I dreamed about it.

"Wake up, Luke," said my mother. "Drink your juice."

It was the next morning. I had just about given up having breakfast with her since Captain Billy had moved in. It was too much to bear.

"You look like you had a bad night," said Captain Billy.

I didn't say anything.

"Can't you answer me, boy?" he asked. "I said something to you. Don't you have any manners at all?"

"Oh, Luke never talks much in the morning, Bill," said Mom. "I gave up trying a long time ago."

"You're too easy on the boy, Mary," said the captain. "He's old enough to know better."

"So are you, Captain," I said.

"Enough of that smart talk," said Captain Billy.

"Please stop," said my mother. "Luke, please be nice to our guest."

"Nice!" I couldn't take it any longer.

"If we were any nicer, we would give him all our money. We've given him a place to live, a job, food, even clothes. I don't see how we could be any nicer," I yelled.

My mother just looked at Captain Billy. I could see they had talked about me. Mom probably couldn't understand why I was acting this way. I had never done it before.

"I'll clear the table, Mary," said Captain Billy. "Why don't you and Luke go in the other room and talk."

"Talk? Talk about what?" I asked.

"I'll tell you in the living room, dear," said my mother.

All of a sudden, I was more afraid than I had ever been before.

"Luke, Bill has asked me to marry him," said my mother.

I had been afraid of something like this. My stomach started jumping up and down.

"What did you say?" I asked.

"I told him I would think about it."

At least she would think about it. I started to feel better.

"I don't know how you could even think of it," I said.

"I know you don't like him," said Mom. "I don't understand why. After all, he was your friend first."

"It's too long a story," I said.

"Anyway, you're thinking about it from your standpoint," she said. "But think of it from mine."

"What do you mean?"

"Luke, your father's been dead a long time. I'm getting older. Someday you'll leave home and get married. I don't want to live the rest of my life alone."

"But why does it have to be Captain Billy?" I asked. "There are lots of other men."

"He's the first one who's asked me out since your father died," said Mom.

"That's because you haven't tried," I said. I thought about it for the first time. "I bet you could meet lots of other people. You just haven't gone anyplace."

"Maybe so," she said, "but I like Bill. He suits me."

"I don't understand it," I said.

"Is there a reason I shouldn't like him? If you know something bad about him, please tell me."

What could I say? Captain Billy was right. How could I tell her she was going out with a ghost? Would she believe me?

"I just don't like him," I said.

"I see. Well, then I'll just have to make up my own mind about Bill, won't I?"

So there I was standing in the first car of the subway all alone. What else could I do? I couldn't let Mom marry Captain Billy. I had to do something. I looked at the light. It seemed much brighter this time. I waited and waited. Nothing happened.

"Come on," I said to myself. "Don't take all night."

It would be really funny if nothing happened when I wanted it to. I looked at the light for so long I almost fell asleep.

Finally, the back of my neck started to feel funny. I turned around. I saw a thin gray shadow in the car.

"Who are you?" I said. "Where did you come from?"

"I'm John Cross," said the shadow. "Who are you?"

"Never mind that. Did you come from the ship Good Hope?"

"How did you know?" asked the shadow. He was getting brighter and brighter.

"Why didn't you come through my body?" I asked.

"I did. You just didn't see me come out," said John. I could see him clearly now. He was a young man dressed the same as Captain Billy, in jeans and a striped shirt.

"But the last time somebody came out, his voice came first," I said.

"It all depends on how you hit the light," he said. "Where am I?"

"You're in New York. It's two hundred years later," I said.

"How did that happen?" he asked.

"Time flies when you're having fun," I said.

"What?"

"Never mind. I brought you here for a reason."

"What's that?" he asked. He was looking around. You could tell he still didn't believe anything I said.

"Do you know a man named Captain Billy Hawkins?" I asked.

"Captain Billy? Is he here?"

"Yes," I said.

"Great," he said. "I can't wait to see him!"

Chapter 10

In the Dark

I wanted to get someone to help me get rid of Captain Billy. But all I had done was bring him a friend. What bad luck!

"Did you like Captain Billy?" I asked.

"He was a good captain," John said. "He always let the men do anything they wanted."

"But what about that man he killed?" I asked.

"How do you know about that?" John looked angry. For the first time, I felt frightened.

"Oh, Captain Billy told me," I said. "We have no secrets from each other."

"We were supposed to keep quiet about it, but as long as the captain told you, I guess it's all right," he said.

"Did you help him?" I asked.

"Of course," he said. "The man was a trouble-maker from the first minute he came on board."

I was feeling sick. I had brought another killer into the light. I decided to change the subject.

"How did you get here?" I asked. "Is it the light that does it?"

"Sure. We catch the light in waves. If you hit it just right, you can ride the light wave into the future. But it isn't easy. Very few of us make it."

"Where were you before you got the light?" I asked.

"In the darkness. It's terrible. Every now and then you get a chance at some light. But most of the time you're trying to get out, feeling your way around and bumping into other people."

"Your whole world is dark?" I asked.

"Not all of it. But the part where I was is almost completely without light."

"How do you get back?" I asked.

"Who wants to go back? I never want to end up in that darkness again."

"It doesn't sound great," I said. "Is there anybody who's been out who's come back?"

"Yes. It's kind of funny. One day they're free and the next they return to the Underdark."

"That's what you call it—the Underdark?" I asked.

"That's the name of the place," he said.

"Why did they come back?"

"If you don't get enough light when you get out, your shadow gets smaller and smaller. You have to make sure you get at least ten hours a day. If you don't, you just aren't in the Light World anymore. You're back in the Underdark."

"Well, I hope things work out for you," I said. The train had reached my stop. I was going to leave this killer on the train. I had enough trouble as it was.

"I won't lose my shadow. That's not going to happen to me. I'm headed for Captain Billy and the bright lights. And you're going to take me there," he said, as he pulled a large knife out of his pocket.

"Of course," I said. "Any friend of Captain Billy's is a friend of mine. You can put that knife away."

"I think I'll keep it," he said. He waved the knife at me.

"Now take me to Billy."

As I walked home with John Cross, I was worried. Captain Billy was bad enough. But he didn't go around pulling knives out of his pocket. He was a killer with a little class. This guy was really bad news. I didn't want my mom anywhere near him. What could I do?

I could wrestle him to the ground. But he had a knife. I couldn't take that chance.

I hoped we would see a cop as we crossed the street. But it was one of those nights when no one's around. We were the only two people walking down the block. I was getting more and more scared. I would have to try and handle this myself.

The only good thing was that no one was home when we got in. Billy was working days that week. I had been upset about that when I found out because I thought he would be able to spend more time with Mom. Now I was glad.

The house was dark. John bumped into a chair.

"Ow!" he yelled.

"Shh!" I said. "Don't wake up my mother. And put that knife in your pocket. You don't want her to see it. Then I'll take you to Billy's room."

I led him to my room, making sure he was behind me. When we got into my room, I closed the door tight.

"Where's Billy?" he asked.

"In here," I said. I opened the closet door and pushed him in. Then I threw all my weight against the door and locked it.

"It's dark in here," he said. "I can't see anything! You tricked me."

He started pounding inside the closet. I moved my heavy dresser against the door.

"Don't send me back. I can't stand it anymore," he cried.

His cries went on for an hour. I turned on my radio to shut out the noise.

At the end of the hour, he sounded much weaker.

"I'll get you for this," he moaned. "I won't have another chance at the light for a long time. But when I do, I'll come after you."

Finally, after three hours, I was brave enough to look into the closet. Nothing was there except the knife—lying on the floor.

By then, Mom and Billy had come home.

"Out pretty late, aren't you?" I said.

"We started dancing and we had such a good time we didn't want to stop," said Mom.

"I'm tired," I said. "I think I'll turn in."

"Don't forget to put a new lightbulb in your closet," said Mom. "That old one burnt out."

"I won't forget," I said. "I'll take care of it tomorrow."

"I need a new bulb, too, Mary," said Captain Billy. "It's for the lamp in the living room."

"I don't wonder," said my mother. "You keep that lamp on all night."

"I like it that way. On the ship we're all used to sleeping with the lights on. It reminds me of my sailing days," he said.

The next day when I looked at Captain Billy over the cornflakes box, I smiled.

"And what are you smiling at?" he asked.

"Nothing," I said. But inside I thought, "Now I know how to get rid of you. But you're much stronger than John Cross. You've been exposed to more light from the X ray. I need someplace very dark that you can't get out of."

What I didn't realize is that while I was planning to do away with Captain Billy, he had his own plans to take care of me.

PART

2

Chapter 11

Maybe

It was around this time that I met Jack Conley. He had a woodworking shop on Eighth Avenue. I didn't usually walk that way, but that day I had to pick up some shoes from the shoe repair shop.

When I saw what was in Jack's window, I stopped dead in my tracks. It was a beautiful table made out of a solid piece of wood. It was as smooth as glass. The grain of the wood went from deep red to pale rose.

I stared at the table for a long time. In fact, I looked for so long that Jack came outside. He was a big man, with red hair and the largest hands I've ever seen.

"It's a beauty, isn't it?" he said.

"Who made it?" I asked.

"I did," he said.

"I wish I could make something like that."

"How good are you with your hands?" he asked.

"I don't know. I've never tried anything like this."

"Well, let's find out," he said.

I found out later that Jack's son had died three years before in a car crash. His son was a little older than me. I think maybe that's why Jack started talking to me. But before I left, we had really hit it off.

The shop was filled with all kinds of wonderful wood. Jack showed me all of them—dark rich woods from Africa and Brazil and red and yellow woods from the U.S. Power tools hung from the walls. There was a long table to work on. The place smelled like the middle of a pine forest.

"We'll start on this," he said, as he handed me a piece of pine.

First, he showed me how to use the tools to cut the wood into the shape I wanted. Then, I learned how to sand it and smooth it. We were going to oil it when a man came into the shop.

"Hi, Jack," he said. "Is my table ready?"

"Sure. Give me a hand, Luke," Jack said.

By the time we had wrapped the table and carried it out to the man's truck, it was time for me to go to the hospital.

"Thanks for everything," I said. "I've got to go to work now."

"Where do you work?" he asked.

"At Memorial Hospital. I'm on the cleaning crew," I said.

"Do you like it?" he asked.

"It's a job," I said. "I can't say more than that."

"Well, you really did seem to enjoy working with wood."

"It's great," I said.

"Why don't you come back in a day or so and we'll do some more," he said.

And that's how Jack and I became friends. With basketball games, seeing Mariel, and working, I was busy. But I made the time to stop by Jack's place at least three or four times a week.

Soon I had made a little table. It was only pine, but I sanded it and smoothed it the way Jack had shown me. Then I rubbed it with oil and let the wood rest for a while.

"That's a nice piece," Jack said. "What are you going to do with it?"

"I'm going to give it to Mom," I said. "I've never been able to give her anything much. I hope she'll like it."

"I'm sure she will," he said.

"I'm not working tonight," I said. "So we'll have a nice dinner, and I'll give it to her then."

"Sounds good," Jack said. "I miss family dinners like that."

I knew about his son, but Jack never talked about a wife.

He must have guessed my question because he said, "I'm divorced. My wife could never forgive me for my son's death."

"But it wasn't your fault," I said.

"I know. But she couldn't forget that I had given him the car. It was an old one. We didn't know the brakes were no good until he tried to stop."

"My father died in a car accident, too," I said. "A drunk driver hit him."

"Sounds like you've had your share of bad luck, too," he said. "It's funny. My wife and I weren't very close before my son's death. After that, there was just nothing left. But I keep remembering the good times we had when my son was little. We used to sit around the dinner table and laugh and talk." His voice trailed off.

"I've got an idea," I said. "Why don't you come with me and see how Mom likes the table? You can stay for dinner. Of course, you'll have to put up with Captain Billy."

"Who's Captain Billy?" he asked.

"I'll fill you in while we're walking."

"I don't want to put your mother out," he said. "After all, I don't want to just walk in on her."

"It's okay. She likes me to bring my friends home."

"Well, we'll see. I'll walk over with you," he said.

"Fine. And if you don't want to stay, you can always leave."

As we walked, I told him about Captain Billy. Not the truth, of course. I still didn't know Jack that well. I didn't want him to think I was crazy. But I think he got the idea that I didn't like Billy all that much.

When we got to the house, Mom had just gotten home. She hadn't changed from her work clothes yet. She looked good.

"Mom, this is Jack Conley," I said.

"Hello, Jack. I'm Mary Mason," she said.

"I've got a surprise for you, Mom." I handed her the little table.

"Isn't this beautiful!" she said. "Where did you get it?"

When she heard I made it, she couldn't believe it.

"Jack helped me. He's got a shop on Eighth Avenue," I said.

"So that's where you were going so early in the morning," she said. "It's so kind of you to help Luke."

"Your son's got a real talent for woodworking," Jack said. "It's a pleasure to work with him."

"Mom, can Jack stay for dinner?" I asked.

"Sure," Mom said.

"Now, Mrs. Mason, I don't want to put you on the spot," Jack said.

"I'd be delighted to have you stay. And please call me Mary."

"All right, Mary," Jack said. "If you're sure it's no trouble."

"What's trouble?" Captain Billy pushed open the door. He had an armful of heavy books.

"Oh, Bill," said Mom. "This is Jack Conley. He's been helping Luke with woodworking. Look at this table Luke made."

"I see," said Captain Billy.

"I'll go start dinner," said Mom. "Jack's eating with us tonight." She went into the kitchen.

Captain Billy walked around the table.

"Not bad," he said. He threw the books onto my table.

One of the legs fell apart.

"But a little shaky," he said, picking up the books and putting them on a chair.

I was ready to throw a punch at Captain Billy. But Jack put his hand on my shoulder.

"I'll help you fix it, Luke," he said.

At dinner, Captain Billy was quiet. He kept looking at Jack and then at Mom.

They were having a great time. Just as I had hit it off with Jack, so did Mom.

"Do you feel like more chicken, Jack?" she asked.

"I feel more like a turkey," he said. "I've eaten so much I'm stuffed."

It was a silly joke but we all laughed. All of us except Captain Billy.

Over coffee and chocolate cake, Mom asked Jack about his work. He talked about the desk and chair he was making.

"I'm using birds-eye maple. It's a wood that's golden brown with little brown spots in it. I'm making the desk so it curves around. And I'm putting in small slots for pens and pencils," he said.

"It sounds beautiful," said Mom.

"Why don't you walk up to the shop with Luke someday and see it?" Jack asked.

"I'd love to," said Mom.

"I should think you might be too busy, Mary," said Captain Billy. "After all, if we're getting married, you're going to have a lot of things to do."

Mom looked surprised, as if she had just woken up from a dream.

"Anytime you have a minute," said Jack, "I'll be happy to see you and show you around the shop. Now let me help you with the dishes."

"That would be wonderful," she said. I let Jack do it even though normally I would be the one to help her. Captain Billy never lifted a hand to help with cooking or the dishes. He said it was women's work.

"Great dinner, Mary," said Captain Billy.

"Thank you, Bill," she said. She and Jack went into the kitchen to wash the dishes.

Captain Billy and I were left alone.

"How about a little TV, Captain?" I asked. I was feeling pretty good. "Maybe we can find an Elvis movie."

He just stared at me.

"What's the matter?" I asked. "Can't you answer me, boy?"

"Don't think I'm not on to what you're doing," he said.

"What?" I asked. But I couldn't help smiling.

"Your mother's going to marry me," he said. "Get that through your thick head."

"She hasn't said yes, yet."

"Just don't try anything. Or I'll take care of you."

"Like I'm really scared."

But Captain Billy had a strange look in his eyes. I tried to hide it, but he did scare me a little.

He picked up the books he had dropped on my table. As he did, I saw part of the title of one of them: "Mental Illness in Young Adults." He walked off to his room.

Maybe Captain Billy was just trying to bluff me. But I knew I'd have to be careful around him. I heard Mom and Jack laughing in the kitchen. Maybe I wouldn't have to do too much. Maybe things would work out by themselves. Maybe I wouldn't be seeing Captain Billy around anymore. Maybe.

Chapter 12

Free

Meanwhile, I wasn't willing to leave everything to chance. Neither was Mariel. She kept on looking for some sort of magic that would help us get rid of Captain Billy.

I had told her what happened with John Cross.

"So now we know they need light to live," she said.

"Too bad I didn't know that when Captain Billy first appeared," I said. "I would have put him in a closet for a week to make sure he went back to the Underdark."

"And after he got that big dose of X-ray, he became super strong," she said.

"That's what did it," I agreed.

"But why did Captain Billy come through you? And you made John Cross come out, too. There must be something about you that makes it happen."

"I don't know," I said. "All I know is I'm not looking at any light for a long time. In fact, now that warm weather is here, I'm going to wear sunglasses all the time."

"Good idea," said Mariel. "By the way, I'm working on something now that might help us."

"Can you tell me about it?" I asked.

"Not yet. Let me find out more about it first."

I tried to drag it out of her, but she wouldn't tell. So I left it alone.

In the meantime, I wore my sunglasses every place I went. I even put them on first thing in the morning.

"Why are you wearing sunglasses to breakfast?" Mom asked.

"My eyes hurt a little bit," I said. "I think I've been reading too much. I want to rest them."

Mom just looked at me. She knows reading too much isn't a problem for me.

Her voice rose. "Is anything the matter?" she asked. I could hear she was getting worried. Her voice always gets higher when she's worried.

"Everything's fine," I said.

Captain Billy came into the kitchen and sat down.

"I hear people on drugs wear sunglasses all the time," he said, smiling. "Hides their eyes. You can always tell by the eyes, they say, if someone's on drugs."

"Luke would never do such a thing," Mom said. Her voice shook. "Would you, Luke?"

"Of course not," I said. I took off the glasses.

"See, my eyes are fine," I said.

But Captain Billy had planted a seed in Mom's mind. After that, she kept giving me worried looks.

I couldn't put on my sunglasses in the house. So I waited until I got to the hospital to do it.

At the hospital, I bumped into Billy all the time. He was on nights again. I tried to stay away from him. But sometimes I could feel him watching me. It was creepy.

He had made friends with some of the older guys. He liked to take his break with them. They would drink coffee and play a few hands of cards. They were always laughing about something. They seemed to enjoy Billy.

While Billy was digging into the hospital, I was making plans to get out. It happened like this.

I finally got Mom to go up to Jack's shop with me. We had a great time. He showed her what he did and what he was working on. She loved the desk. I did too. Jack had shaped the wood into a perfect half circle. Now he was busy carving the slots. He showed Mom how he would make designs in the wood to decorate it.

When he had finished showing Mom around, he invited us out for coffee.

"Oh, thank you, Jack," said Mom. "But I really have a lot to do. I have to get back home."

"I'd like to sit down and talk to you, Mary, with Luke," Jack said. "It's important."

"Come on, Mom," I said. "You have time for coffee. It won't take long." I didn't know what Jack was going to say, but I liked him and wanted Mom to like him too.

After we sat down in the coffee shop, Jack said: "I don't know if you know much about me, Mary. I had a wife. She divorced me. I had a son. He died."

"Jack, you don't have to tell us this," said Mom.

"I do. Because I want to tell you that my life went off track after my son died. We had planned that he would come into the business with me. He loved to work with wood just like Luke. After he died, I wasn't sure I could work with wood again. I thought about selling my shop."

He stopped and drank some coffee.

"I can understand that," said Mom. "I didn't know what to do when my husband died."

"Then you do understand," said Jack. "Finally, I decided I had to go on living. But I didn't enjoy anything. Nothing was fun. Everything was hard. Then one day I met Luke. And some of the fun came back."

"Luke's a wonderful boy," said Mom. "But I'm not sure what you mean."

"Luke has a lot of talent for woodworking," he said. "I'd like to take him into my business. I can teach him what I know while he helps me. He'll get paid of course. And someday, maybe he'll want to buy into the business."

"That's very nice of you," said Mom. "I never really thought about woodworking for Luke. I always thought he might go to college."

"He could still do that if he wanted to," Jack said. "He could take classes at night."

"You haven't asked me what I think," I said. These two were planning my future without even talking to me.

"What do you think?" asked Jack.

"I think it would be great. I really like working with my hands. I've never been very interested in studying, Mom. You know that," I said.

"I sure do," said Mom.

"Tell you what," said Jack. "Let's give it a try for six months. If you don't like it after that, or we don't get along, either one of us can back out."

"Fine," I said. "I'll leave the hospital tonight."

Mom shook her head. "That's not right, Luke. You have to give them more time than that. Tell them you're leaving in a week, so they have time to get someone else for your job."

"You listen to your mother," said Jack. "Now that you're working for me you have to act like a businessman. Treat the hospital right."

I was as happy as I had been in a long time. I had a great job ahead of me. Mom and Jack seemed to be hitting it off. I couldn't wait to tell Mariel.

She seemed a little disappointed at the beginning.

"But what about college, Luke?" she asked. "I thought we would go together when we had saved up enough money."

"I can go at night. Jack thinks it's a good idea, too. I have to learn how to run a business. Someday, I'll own part of the shop. Conley and Mason. Won't that be great?"

"I'm just glad you're happy and that you're getting out of the hospital. What a dead-end job!"

"I can hardly wait to leave," I said.

I took Mariel to the shop that evening. Jack had gone home. But we could look in the lighted window and see some of the pieces he was making. The street was quiet. No one was around. So we stayed for a long time, just looking. Mariel loved the table.

"Someday I'll make you one just like it," I said.

"That's a promise," she said. "I can understand now why you want to do this. It's not just working with wood, it's really making something."

"That's it," I said. "I feel free when I do it. As if I could do anything."

But we had forgotten that there might be someone who wasn't happy to see me leave the hospital, someone who wanted to keep an eye on me at all times.

"I don't think this woodworking job is such a good idea, Mary," Captain Billy said that night. "After all, Luke needs a steady hand. I won't be able to look after him if he's not at the hospital."

"Who needs you to look after me?" I yelled. "I've been looking after myself for a long time."

Captain Billy went right on, as if I hadn't spoken.

"And we don't know anything about this Jack, do we? I mean he's not a family friend or someone your husband knew. He's just a man who's taken a liking to Luke."

"Yeah, he doesn't come into people's homes and start living with them and taking their money and their food," I said. "He's strange that way."

Captain Billy glared at me. Then he said, "I really think Luke is better off at the hospital with me."

Mom listened to him. "You have a point, Bill," she said. "But I think Luke really needs to do something else. He can't work at the hospital all his life. He needs different kind of work."

"The hospital is good steady work, Mary," he said. "He'll never be out of a job. He'll always be able to get good health care. This woodworking place—who knows if it'll be there tomorrow? Who knows what kind of money he'll make? Who knows what kind of man this Jack is?"

"I have to take a chance, Mom, " I said. "I can't mop floors the rest of my life. I'll go crazy if I do."

"I think Luke should try it," said Mom. "If it doesn't work out, he can always go back to the hospital."

"Very well," said Captain Billy. "I tried. I only want to help the poor fatherless boy. After all, it's hard for a woman to raise a child alone. But I guess my help isn't needed."

Then, of course, Mom had to tell Billy he was wanted. And that his ideas were good. And that she liked him helping her. And that it was hard for her alone. I couldn't stand to listen so I went off to bed. Captain Billy made me sick.

Chapter 13

All Wet

Some of the people at the hospital seemed sorry that I was leaving. The ones I worked with during the day even gave me a little going-away party with cake and ice cream. They promised to stop by the shop and say hello.

Dr. Rogers still looked at me now and then. I was glad to be seeing the last of him.

I was on the night shift that last week. As I pushed my mop around, I kept looking at the hospital, thinking, "This is the last time I'll be doing this." I was so happy.

Captain Billy was working at night, too. But he had stayed away from me after that night when he had told my mother I should stay at the hospital. I guess he was mad he hadn't won her over to his way of thinking.

Three nights before I was supposed to leave I bumped into him and Dr. Rogers.

"Ah, Luke," said Captain Billy. "We were just talking about you."

"Bill tells me you're not feeling too well, Luke," Dr. Rogers said.

"I feel fine," I said. "Now if you'll excuse me, I have work to do."

"Are you sure you feel all right?" Dr. Rogers asked. "Bill tells me you're very angry sometimes, and your mother can't control you."

"Bill should mind his own business," I said. I couldn't help it. I was getting very angry.

"You see what I mean, Doctor," Bill said. "He's always angry. His mother needs me to help with him. She just can't handle him."

I dropped my mop and started to go after Captain Billy.

Dr. Rogers stepped in between us.

"Settle down, now," he said.

"I think he should see you, Doctor, to learn how to deal with his anger," said Captain Billy.

"I'll deal with you later," I said.

Dr. Rogers was looking at me as if I would be his next case. I tried to cool it.

"Thank you, Doctor, and thank you, Captain Billy, for caring. But I'm just fine," I said.

"Why do you call him Captain?" asked Dr. Rogers.

"You see what I told you," said Captain Billy. "He's got some strange ideas about me. Thinks I'm a sea captain who lived hundreds of years ago."

"No, not at all," I said. "I just call him captain for fun."

"So you know he's a real man named Bill," said Dr. Rogers.

"Of course," I said. "Now I really do have to get back to work."

"Yes, lad," said Captain Billy. "I'll come help you in a minute."

I walked away before I could tell Captain Billy I didn't need his kind of help. He caught up with me a few minutes later.

"I told your mother you needed me around," he said. "Otherwise, you might get into trouble."

"Captain, you keep fooling around like this, and you'll have trouble and more from me," I said.

"I can stop now," he said. "All you have to do is tell Jack you're not going to work for him."

"Why should I do that?" I asked.

"I don't want that fellow around my house," he said. "He's too friendly with your mother."

"Your house," I said. "Your house. Since when is it your house? Since when do you tell me and my mother what to do and who to see?"

"You'd better listen to me," he said. "You don't want to be locked up, do you?"

"You couldn't do it," I said. "Besides, I'll be out of here in just a few days. Once I'm gone, I'll never come back to this hospital—ever. You won't be able to drag me."

Captain Billy just smiled.

"And you're not married to my mother, yet. In fact, I don't think you ever will be. I'm betting that she gets rid of you as soon as she gets to know Jack better."

"Why would she want that stupid carpenter when she could have a real man?" he asked. "You're way off."

"I don't know, Captain. Once I'm working at the shop, she'll have lots of reasons for visiting. After all, it's only two blocks away from the house."

"We've been talking about a date for the wedding," Captain Billy said. "How would you like to be my best man?"

"Over your dead body," I said.

"We'll see, boy, won't we?" said Captain Billy. "We'll see."

I knew Captain Billy was up to some dirty tricks. What could I do? I had no idea what he was planning. But the first thing I did was talk to my mother.

"Mom, have you and Bill set a wedding date?" I asked.

"No, Luke, I haven't even said I would marry Bill yet. I'm still making up my mind," she said.

"Good. Very good. Take your time," I said. "Take all the time in the world."

"I will take my time. Bill is a good man. But I want to be sure before I get married again. You and he get along so badly I really wonder about it," she said.

"I don't want you to marry him. That's for sure," I said.

"We'll see. But I'm not even near setting a date," she said.

That was a load off my mind. Next, I had to try and make some plans myself.

I talked to Mariel on the phone that night.

"You know that little necklace I wear," she said.

"Yes. It's supposed to keep you safe," I said. "Not that I really believe in that stuff.

"My Mom does. She got it for me."

"Where did she get it?"

"It's a special store. They have spells and charms for everything. And saints who are supposed to protect you," she said.

"I think we should go there together. Let's see if we can find something to protect you against Captain Billy. I've been trying to find something on the Internet, but I haven't come up with anything yet. Let's see what the store has."

"I guess we should," I said. "I don't know what Captain Billy's planning. But I need some protection."

"I'll meet you tomorrow morning," she said. "The library doesn't open until one. We'll have plenty of time."

She led me to the little shop the next day. It was filled with all kinds of little bottles and statues of saints. The bottles were filled with what looked like water. There were brightly-colored pictures on the walls. Necklaces like Mariel's were on the counter. The owner came out. He spoke Spanish, so Mariel talked to him.

"I told him you were in danger," she said. "He wants to know what from?"

"Can you tell him I'm in danger from a ghost?" I asked.

"I'll try," she said. She started talking again to the owner. I was afraid he would laugh or throw us out of the place. But he listened to Mariel. Then he gave her a bottle of water.

"He said this is good for getting rid of ghosts. Just throw a few drops on the ghost and he'll go away," she said.

"Okay," I said. "It's worth a try."

I bought the water and a man's necklace like Mariel's for myself. We looked around some more before we left.

"Look, here's something for headaches. Here's something for pain," she said.

"What a great place," I said. "I hope this works."

I planned to try the water when I got to work that night. It would be easy to pretend to spill some on Captain Billy. I put the necklace on. I needed all the help I could get.

That night I slipped the water in my pocket before I went to work. I got out my mop and started to clean the floors. Soon I ran into Captain Billy. He was working down the hall.

I headed straight for him. I took out the bottle and took off the cap. I was ready to spill the water on him, when something hit me hard.

"Watch out, Luke," said Susan. "I nearly ran

you down with my cart." She went rushing down the hall.

I looked down at the bottle. All the water had spilled on my pants.

Captain Billy looked up. "What happened to you?" he asked. "You're all wet."

"Just got some water from the mop on me," I said. "Nothing more."

I threw the bottle in the glass can and walked on. So much for getting rid of Captain Billy with special water. I would have to find another way.

Looking back at Billy, I saw him shake his head. He stared at me. What was he thinking? I wish I knew.

Chapter 14

A Bad Dream

It was hard falling asleep that night. I tossed and turned trying to get comfortable. Once I did fall asleep, I had one bad dream after another.

In one dream Captain Billy was chasing me around the hospital with a knife. In another, he was marrying Mom and there was nothing I could do to stop him. When the minister said, "Is there anyone here who wants to speak against these people getting married?", I wanted to talk, but I couldn't say anything. I had lost my voice.

I woke up from that one shouting. Mom called out, "Luke, is that you?"

"Yes, Mom. I just had a bad dream," I answered.

"Okay." She went back to sleep.

But I couldn't. I shut my eyes. I tried to count sheep, although that's never done me any good. Finally, I got up and went into the kitchen. I thought I might wake Captain Billy, since he slept on the couch in the living room. But I didn't hear a sound, and his lamp was not on.

I turned on the kitchen light. I'd have some milk and cookies. Maybe I'd be able to sleep after that. I sat there for a while, eating and reading the newspaper. It was about four in the morning when I finished. I was just thinking about going back to bed when I heard a noise. It sounded like someone at the door.

I turned off the kitchen light. If it was someone breaking into the house, I wanted to be able to surprise him in the dark.

Then I heard the noise of the key turning in the lock. Who else had a key to our house?

Someone came in. He walked very quietly. There was a little light from the window, and I could see him if I looked hard. He went over to the couch. It looked as if he was taking off his clothes. I heard his shoes hit the floor. He lay down on the couch. It was Captain Billy.

He never looked my way. He must have thought that Mom and I were sleeping. Soon I heard him snoring. Very quietly, I went back to my room.

This was interesting. What was Captain Billy doing out so late? Why did he come in so quietly? What was going on?

The next morning Billy turned up for breakfast. I would have thought he would sleep in, but there he was at the table. He seemed very happy. I hadn't seen him so happy in a long time.

"Today's your last day at the hospital, isn't it, Luke?" he asked.

"Yep, it is. I can't wait to start working with Jack," I said.

"Well, I want to wish you luck," he said.

"That's big of you, Captain," I said. "I thought you didn't like the idea of me working with him."

"I've changed my mind. I think it's fine," he said.

Mom smiled. "I'm glad to hear that, Bill. I think it's a good idea myself. I'm glad we think alike."

"Oh, yes," said Captain Billy. "We think alike about a lot of things. That's why we're such a good match."

"More juice, Luke?" Mom asked.

"No, I'd like to get over to Jack's early so we can start planning what I'm going to do," I said. I could hardly wait to get to the shop.

"Say hello for me," Mom said.

Captain Billy just smiled. He seemed to think something was very funny.

But I couldn't be bothered thinking about him today. I was so excited. I was starting a new life.

I almost ran the two blocks to Jack's shop. It was a nice sunny day. But as I got closer and closer to the shop, the air started to smell funny, like something was burning.

Then I saw fire engines parked in front of Jack's store.

"Oh, no," I yelled. I raced the rest of the way almost crying.

Two firefighters were carrying out the beautiful desk. Only it wasn't beautiful anymore. Instead of being golden brown it was burnt black. Half of it had been eaten away by the fire.

I looked at what was left of the shop. It, too, was black and filled with glass and water.

I ran over to one of the firefighters carrying the desk. "Where's the owner?" I asked.

He paid no attention to me. I pulled on his sleeve.

"What?" he yelled.

"Where's the owner? Is he okay?" I cried.

"He's okay. I don't know where he is now." The firefighters threw the desk into a heap of garbage.

Then I saw Jack. He was standing inside the shop, just looking around. He was covered with dirt and soot.

I ran to him. "Jack, I'm so sorry. What happened?"

He looked at me for a moment. "Oh, Luke, I forgot to call you. I got here at eight. The fire had already been going for a while. It looks like there's nothing left to save. I'm wiped out."

"But Jack, isn't there anything you can do?" I asked.

"I don't know. My insurance will cover most of this. But I don't know if I have the heart to go on."

"You have to, Jack. It would be terrible if you gave up now," I said. I knew how long it had taken him to feel good again after his son's death.

"We'll see. In the meantime, you'd better keep your hospital job for the time being."

"But I can leave if you need me," I said.

"I need some time alone to think. Luke, I like your company. But I have to think about what to do. Too much has happened to me lately. I need some time away."

"Where will you be?" I asked.

"I don't know. But I have to get away for a while."

"Okay," I said. "But please call me. Let me know how you are. I'll worry about you."

"You're a good kid," he said. We shook hands and I left him there, looking at the ashes of his work.

As for me, all my dreams had gone up in smoke. I had been so excited about working with Jack and making beautiful things. Now I might spend the rest of my life cleaning floors in the hospital. Then I got mad at myself. Here I was feeling sorry for me when I should have been thinking about Jack. He had lost a lot more than I had.

I went to the hospital later and asked them if I could keep my job. They said okay, and I was back where I started.

Later, I told Mom and Mariel. They both felt terrible for Jack.

"Is there anything we can do?" Mom asked. "Let's call and see how he's doing."

But there was no answer on Jack's phone. He had shut off his machine.

"Where can he be?" Mom asked.

"He said he needed time away," I said. "He'll be back." I didn't know if I really believed that Jack would come back, but I had to hope.

Mom told Captain Billy when he came home.

"So, Luke, you'll be staying at the hospital," he said. "Good, good."

"I thought you said that working with Jack was a good idea," I said.

"I only said that because you seemed so set on it," he said. "It's too bad about the shop. But these things happen."

He yawned and stretched.

"I'm really tired tonight," he said. "I think I'll turn in early."

I heard nothing more about the fire for a week. Then I picked up the newspaper and read the headlines: "FIRE AT WOOD SHOP WAS SET."

It seems the insurance company had searched through the shop and found some things that made it look like the fire had been started on purpose. One of the things they had found were matches from a place called The Blue Bridge. The police were looking for Jack. They thought he might have done it for the insurance money.

"It's a good thing you didn't go to work for that fellow," Captain Billy said. "Looks like he set that fire. I was right all the time. I thought there was something funny about him."

"He didn't set that fire," I said. "Why would he do that? I was going to work for him the next day. Why bother to ask me to work for him if he was going to burn the place down?"

"You never know," said Captain Billy. "Some of these fellows are funny that way. Maybe he asked you so it would look good for the police. He was just trying to use you."

"I'll never believe that," I said. "Never."

"Suit yourself," said Billy. "What do you think, Mary?"

"I don't know what to think," she said. "He seemed like such a nice man. I'm sure the police are wrong."

"I think they've got the right man," said Billy.

And that's all Captain Billy would say. Of course, he didn't like Jack. The police looked for him and couldn't find him. I kept calling his house, but there was no answer. I couldn't even walk past the shop anymore. It was all boarded up. It looked terrible.

Life went on. I played basketball. I saw Mariel. I worked at the hospital. But all the fun seemed to have gone out of things.

Captain Billy left me alone pretty much. Now that Jack was gone, he didn't watch me so closely. But he and Mom still did a lot of things together. And, of course, I saw him at work.

One night Billy was leaving the cafeteria with his friends when I passed by. I was getting some coffee for Susan.

He lit up a cigar. Every now and then he would smoke one. I hated the smell.

"Come on, Bill," said the guard. "You know

there's no smoking here."

"Okay, okay," he said. He put the cigar out in the sand tray. Then he tried to throw the empty matchbook into the garbage can.

He missed and walked out the door.

"Bad throw, Captain Billy," I said. I picked it up, wanting to make the throw and show him up. Something made me look at it. I froze. The matches were from The Blue Bridge.

I remembered that Captain Billy hadn't gotten home until very late the night of the fire. He didn't like Jack. He was afraid that Mom liked Jack too much. Had Billy hated Jack enough to set fire to his shop? Was Billy the kind of man who would do something like that? I thought so. Captain Billy had killed a man and he had also killed my friend's hopes and my dreams. I couldn't do anything about the man Billy had killed. But I could make sure that Billy didn't get away with what he had done to Jack and me.

I should have waited until I cooled down. I should have remembered I couldn't really prove that Billy had set the fire.

I should have counted to ten, and then counted to ten again. But I did none of these things.

Instead, I raced up to Billy, grabbed him and started hitting him. He was taken by surprise, so I was able to get a few good licks in even though he was much bigger and heavier than I am.

His friends tried to help him.

"Just get the doctor!" he yelled. "Get Doctor Rogers!"

He grabbed my arm and twisted it behind me as they left us alone.

"I know all about you," I cried. "You set the fire! You burned Jack's place down. Wait until I tell the cops. This is no two-hundred-year-old crime. Everybody will care about this one!"

"You must be out of your mind," he said. "I had nothing to do with that fire."

I struggled to get my right arm free.

"Then how come you came in so late that night?" I asked. "And why do you have matches from The Blue Bridge?"

I held up the match book in my left hand. He tore the match book out of my hand.

"Where did you get those? Have you been snooping in my things?" he asked.

"You're so dumb, Captain," I said. "You just dropped them when you put out your cigar."

"How do you know I dropped them? They could be anybody's."

"I saw you," I said.

"And who's going to believe the word of a madman?" he asked.

"What's going on here?" Dr. Rogers came running over.

Captain Billy still held me.

"It's just as we feared, Doctor," he said. "The boy's had a breakdown. He started calling me

Captain again. He hit me and shouted all kinds of things about me."

"Doctor, this man is out to get me," I said. "He's trying to hurt me. He burned down the shop of one of my friends."

Doctor Rogers didn't even listen to me.

"Yes," he said, "we were afraid of this. I'll give him a shot to quiet him down."

"No," I screamed. "There's nothing wrong with me. It's him, Captain Billy. He's the one."

"It's a bad case, Doctor, isn't it?" asked Billy.

"I'm afraid so," said Doctor Rogers. "We may have to sign him into the hospital for a few days. I'll get another doctor to see him after that."

I tried to break free, but Captain Billy was too strong.

"You can't do this," I cried. "I'm not the one with a problem. I'm really all right. Doctor, please listen to me."

But Doctor Rogers just plunged a needle into my arm, and soon it was all I could do to keep my head up. Dr. Rogers said he was going to talk to some other doctors. I was left in a wheelchair with Captain Billy.

Before I fell asleep, I saw Captain Billy smiling. I thought I heard him say, "You've got to learn something, Luke. It doesn't pay to get angry at your enemies. It just slows you up. You should learn from me. I don't get mad, I get even."

Chapter 15

Take It Easy

I woke up in a cell all alone. I was lying on a small, hard bed. I sat up. My head started to hurt, and I felt sick. I looked around. There were no windows. A single light was on above me. The walls were covered with mattresses.

"Hello, " I yelled. "Where is everybody?"

No one answered.

"Hello. Help! Help!" No one came. Finally, I gave up and lay down again. I was very tired, more tired than I had ever been in my life. It was hard to move. I felt as if I was doing everything in slow motion. It was hard to think. I knew what had happened, but I wasn't sure where I was.

Was I still in the hospital? Or had Captain Billy and Doctor Rogers taken me somewhere else? I knew I should be afraid, but it was hard to feel anything. I just didn't seem to care about anything. Dr. Rogers must have given me something very powerful to make me feel this way. All I wanted to do was sleep. But I knew I shouldn't.

I was in danger. I knew that much. I fought against closing my eyes again.

"How are you feeling?" I jumped up. I must have fallen asleep again.

"Who are you?" I asked.

"I'm Doctor Ramirez," he said. "I'm covering for Doctor Rogers."

"Where am I?"

"You're in Metro Hospital," he said.

"So they did it," I said.

"Excuse me?" said Doctor Ramirez.

"Doctor Rogers and Captain Billy. They got me locked up with the crazies," I said.

"They're just trying to help you. You are in the Psychiatric Ward, that's true. And you need some rest and some treatment."

"Doctor, there's nothing wrong with me," I said.

"That's not what Doctor Rogers says."

"Why does he say I'm here?" I asked.

"Why don't you ask him?" he suggested. "I'm just here to check on you."

"Come on, Doctor. I'd like to know what he said."

"Most people are here because they're a danger to themselves and to others," he said.

"Believe me, I'm not dangerous," I said. "Can't you let me go? I'd really like to go home."

"I wish I could. We've got too many in here as it is. The place is overcrowded. But you have to stay here for 72 hours," he said.

"Then I can go home?"

"Then you have to go before a group of doctors. They'll ask you all kinds of questions. If they think you're okay, they'll let you go home," he said.

"That's three days," I said. "I have to stay in this cell for three days?"

"No, if you behave okay, they'll let you go into the ward tomorrow. The cells are just for the troublemakers and the people who can't control themselves."

"Doctor, you've probably heard bad things about me," I said. "It was a setup. I haven't done anything. But there is one man who's out to get me."

"Captain Billy, right?" he asked.

"Oh, you know him?" I asked.

"Doctor Rogers told me you had a thing about him. I've never met the man."

"Doctor Rogers likes him," I said. "But Captain Billy has killed a man. He set fire to my friend's shop. Now he's trying to get rid of me."

"Lots of people in here think someone's out to get them," he said. "Why don't you get some rest? Lunch will be along soon. Eat something and try and take it easy."

"You have to believe me," I said. "Someone's got to believe me."

"If you ever want to get out of here, you'll give up this Captain Billy thing," he said. "I've got to go now."

"Wait a minute." I looked down at my feet. I had no shoes on. "Where are my shoes? And my belt?"

"They took them away. They always do," he said.

"Why?"

"So you don't hurt yourself," he said. "I'm late for my rounds. See you later."

He shut the door and locked it. I was alone again with my anger.

For the next two days, I learned what life was like all alone in a cell. I don't suggest you try it. When they finally let me out of the cell, I thought I'd have someone to talk to. Forget it. Most of the people I saw were too out of it to talk. Like me, they had been given so many pills and shots, they had trouble staying awake.

Those who were awake were another story. There was one girl who played her CDs all the time as loud as she could. She sang along with them, making up songs to tell the doctors how well she was and how they should let her go.

Another guy only wanted to play Ping-Pong with you. If you won, he cried. But most just wanted to watch TV or sit around looking into space. It was too much trouble to do anything else.

I felt better than most of them because I wasn't taking my pills. I found I could hide them when I drank the water. The first time I tried to fool the nurse, I was worried. But then I saw she didn't really look at me when she gave me the water. As Dr. Ramirez had said, there were just too many people in the place to take care of. After that, it was easy.

But when you came right down to it, no matter what I did, I wasn't free. I couldn't go outside. I couldn't go to the gym and play a game of basketball. I couldn't decide to see a movie. I had no rights. I couldn't get up and leave. I was trapped.

The second day I was there they let Mom visit me.

"Luke," she cried, "how are you?" She had tears in her eyes.

"I'm fine, Mom. This is a big mistake. I just want to get out of here," I said. "Please take me home."

"The doctor says you need some rest and treatment," she said.

"Mom, they don't do anything for me here," I said. "All they do is give you pills that make you sleep."

She looked troubled. But Captain Billy had done a good job on her.

"I feel so bad," she said. "You must have been feeling terrible all along. Don't worry. When you get out, Bill and I will take care of you."

"Bill!" I shouted. "That's who got me into this in the first place. He's been planning this all along. First, he burns down Jack's shop. Then he gets me locked up. You have to get rid of him. He's bad, Mom. I can't even tell you how bad he is."

"Oh, Luke," she said. "They tell me this is part of your illness. Bill is just trying to help you."

"Mom, can't you believe me?"

"You just rest now, Luke. And as soon as they let us, we'll take you home. I'm sorry I upset you. I'd better be going now."

"Mom, please, please," I said. I couldn't say anymore. I was afraid I'd cry.

She hugged and kissed me. And then she was gone. What hope did I have? My own mother didn't believe me.

It was at that point I decided I'd better lie if I ever wanted to get out of there. The next day I would have to see the group of doctors, and I couldn't get mad or tell them the truth if I wanted to be free.

But I didn't know they would set a trap for me.

I took a shower before I went before the group for a hearing. Mom had left some clean clothes for me. They even gave me back my belt and my shoelaces.

The nurse took me down to the room where I would see the doctors. I was shaking before I went in. I was so afraid I would have to stay in the hospital forever.

"Good morning, Luke."

It was a doctor I had never seen before. He and the other doctors were sitting around a big table.

They had me sit at one end.

I looked around and saw Dr. Rogers. He didn't smile but just stared at me.

"I'm Dr. Sylvan, and we'd like to ask you a few questions," the doctor said.

I soon stopped shaking. They asked easy questions. What's your name? Where do you live? Who's the President of the United States?

How much is 10 plus 13? Everyone was soon smiling. It seemed as if they would let me go.

Then Dr. Rogers asked, "Who's Captain Billy?"

One of the other doctors said, "That's not on our list, John."

"I have a reason for asking this question. It's about the boy's state of mind," he said. "Please answer, Luke."

I was trapped. If I said, "I don't know," Dr. Rogers would know I was lying. If I told the truth, no one would believe me. I tried to get around it.

"Captain Billy is an old sea captain who lived two hundred years ago," I said.

"Do you think he's still alive today?" he asked.

I didn't know what to say. Finally, I lied. "No," I said.

"Then why did you call Bill Hawkins, Captain Billy?"

"It was just for fun," I said.

"And was it just for fun when you tried to attack him?" he asked.

"I was angry," I said.

"About what?" he asked.

"I don't want to talk about it," I said.

Dr. Rogers walked to the door and opened it. In walked Captain Billy.

"Hello, Luke," he said. "I hope you're feeling better."

"Who's this?" asked one of the doctors.

"This is Bill Hawkins," said Dr. Rogers. "I brought him here because I'm afraid this boy is very sick. If we let him go, he may hurt someone. Bill is here to tell us about him."

"Well, I hate to say anything against the boy," said Captain Billy. "After all, his mother and I are very close. I think the boy is angry about that. That's the only reason I can think of why he wants to hurt me. He's tried all kinds of ways to get at me, and I do think he's becoming a danger. He tells me I'm a sea captain who lived two hundred years ago, and I killed someone. Then he tells me I set fire to someone's shop. His mother and I are very upset about him."

"You lying . . ." I tried to grab Billy, but some doctors held me back.

"Guard, guard!" they called.

"You see what I mean," said Dr. Rogers. "We can't let him go. He's a danger to at least this man and maybe others."

Two guards came in and took hold of me. As they marched me out, I turned to Captain Billy.

"You'll pay for this," I said.

He just smiled. I could imagine him later talking to my mother.

"I tried my best, Mary," he would say. "But I just couldn't help him."

While everyone was talking at once, Captain Billy said in a quiet voice, "It'll be a long time until I see you again, Luke. They're not going to let you out so fast. They could keep you here up to two years. By that time, a lot of things could change."

I was back in my cell all alone. There was no one who could help me. But I had forgotten about someone. Help was coming very soon.

Chapter 16

A Friend In Need

I lay on my bed in the room. All hope was gone. I kept trying to think of ways to get out but I was stuck. I still wasn't taking my pills, but that didn't help. All it meant was I didn't sleep as much anymore. But since there was nothing to do, I was bored out of my head.

The only thing I could do was pretend not to be angry. Any time I showed any anger at all, they put me in the cell. If I tried acting as if nothing bothered me, they would put me back in the ward, and the chances of escape were much greater there.

So I was pleasant when the guard came with my dinner. He was listening to the ball game on his radio.

"What's the score?" I asked.

"Yankees are leading two-nothing against Boston," he said.

I made sure we had a good talk about baseball before he left. I was certain they had him report on how I was acting.

Sure enough, the next day they moved me back to the ward. This time, I looked around more. This was my chance. The ward was the only place where there was enough freedom to be able to get out.

But this time they made sure my time was filled up. Because I was now there for a longer time, they made out a plan for me. I had to see the doctor for therapy. I had to spend time in the art group. I had to go to a men's group. Most of my time was spent talking about my feelings or listening to other people talk about theirs. I could see that some people were getting the help they needed.

I learned how to talk the talk, but I knew that nobody could help me with my problems because they would never believe me.

I soon saw that those who were the least trouble had the most freedom. Some people even got passes to go out with their friends or family.

I hadn't heard from Mom since I had seen her before the hearing. I figured Billy had filled her head with stuff about leaving me alone to work out my problems. But it still hurt that she didn't come to see me.

So I was surprised when they told me I had a visitor. Was it Mom at last?

"Mariel," I said. "I didn't expect you."

"I came as soon as they would let me," she said. "Luke, you look terrible. What have they done to you?"

111

"I can't tell you the whole story now. There are too many people listening. Let's just make small talk, and maybe I'll be able to get a pass soon. Then I can tell you everything."

"Do you really think people are listening?" she asked, looking around.

"I must admit it seems wild, but I know that Captain Billy and Dr. Rogers are in this together," I said. "Maybe other people are in on it, too. All I know is I have to be very, very careful."

"Okay, you know best," she said. So we talked about the library and her job and some of our friends.

Then the bell rang. Visiting hours were over.

"Thanks for coming," I said. "I haven't seen anyone but Mom since I've been here. And she only came once."

"That's awful," said Mariel. "Do you want me to talk to her?"

"Please don't," I said. "It'll just stir Captain Billy up. Will you come back?"

"Of course. I have to work late tomorrow. But I'll be back on Wednesday."

"I'll see you then," I said. "Please come back. I'm counting on you. And Mariel—thanks!"

She just smiled and waved. I watched her walk away with the rest of the visitors. I thought I had cared about her before when we were going out, but now I could see how important she really was to me. She was the only one who knew the truth about Captain Billy and the only one I trusted to help me. I knew I could hardly last another day here, let alone two years. She was my one chance to get out of here, and I knew she wouldn't let me down.

I counted the hours until her next visit. In the meantime, I was as good as I could be. I let the Ping-Pong guy win. I talked with the guards. I talked with my doctor and even told him how much he was helping me. I started making a basket in the art group. I did everything to try and get a pass. It worked!

When Wednesday came around, I was able to tell Mariel that I had a pass for lunch on Saturday.

"That's good," said Mariel. "I won't work this Saturday. I think I can trade with someone."

"What if you can't?" I asked. This was my one chance.

"Then I'll call in sick," she said.

I had taken a chance and told Mariel what had happened to me at the hearing. I had waited until the main visitors' room was clear, and we had pretended to play checkers. When she heard what Captain Billy had done, she seemed even more angry than I was. I knew I could count on her.

She knew how important it was to show up that day. We had made our plans. It was great to have someone believe me and trust me again.

When Saturday came, I was up early. The guard laughed.

"I haven't seen you get up so early since you got here. Usually, we have to drag you out of bed."

"Today's a big day. I've got a pass for lunch, and my girlfriend's coming to take me out."

"Great! Just make sure you don't forget the time. You've only got three hours. They're very careful about how long you can stay out."

"Don't worry," I said. "I won't forget."

I stood by the door until Mariel came at noon. She was right on time. But I had been waiting since 11:00. I just couldn't sit still.

"Let's go," I said. We smiled at each other. Then we took off.

We walked slowly out of the hospital door. When we left the grounds, we started to run.

We were lucky. A train was waiting in the subway station. We took it and then switched cars three times to make sure no one was following us. Neither of us saw anyone, but it didn't hurt to make sure.

When the train pulled into the Smith Street station, we got off.

I took off my jacket. Mariel pulled a hat out of her bag and put it on. I thought we looked different enough so that if anyone had been following us, they might not notice our change of clothes.

We walked quickly up the street, but not so fast that someone might remember. It was a gloomy day, and only a few people were out. Luck was with us.

Mariel and I ducked into her house.

"I wish I could think of a better place," I said.

"No problem," she said. "No one ever goes down to the basement. If you do hear someone coming, you can always hide."

I looked around. There was a large sofa stored in the corner.

"I can always hide behind that," I said.

"I don't think you'll have to," said Mariel. "I'll bring you some food later on. I'd better go now."

"I'm sorry you have to do this," I said. "It's the only way I can think of to keep you out of it."

"No problem," she said. "When I think of what they did to you, I could spit. I'll be happy to lie for you."

She left and I was alone again. But this time, things were different. I was free of the hospital. I had a safe place to stay and time to think about what to do. No one was trying to fill me with pills that would make me too tired to do anything. I felt like a person again.

In the meantime, Mariel took the train back up to the hospital.

She told me later that she messed up her hair and her clothes, and then she ran into the hospital crying.

"Help! Please help me!" she called.

"What's the matter?" asked the guard.

"I was out with one of your nuts. He tried to attack me. Then he ran away. I never knew he was so crazy."

"Are you all right?" asked the guard.

"Yes," said Mariel. "But I don't know what to do."

"You were with Luke, weren't you? I'll get the doctor," the guard said.

He came running back with Dr. Rogers.

"Who are you?" asked Dr. Rogers.

"I'm a friend of Luke's. My name is Mariel," she said. "We were out for lunch. All of a sudden, he went crazy. He tried to attack me. Then he ran away. I thought I should tell you."

"Where did you lose him?" asked Dr. Rogers.

"On the street," said Mariel. "I'll show you where."

She took Dr. Rogers ten blocks in a different direction.

"I'll call the police," said Dr. Rogers. "He could be anywhere. He's certainly shown that he's dangerous. Maybe he'll try to call you later. Why don't you leave your name, address and phone number? In the meantime, I'll call and warn his family."

I had told Mariel to be sure to give them the right information. Otherwise, they might think she was trying to put one over on them.

So she wrote down her name, address and phone number and then left the hospital.

Later that night, she came down to the basement to visit me.

"I don't think we're out of the woods yet," I said. "Captain Billy is sure to come over here looking for me."

"I'll make him believe me," Mariel said.

"He'll be sure to think I'm hiding," I said. "You're going to have to put on a very good act for him."

"Don't worry," she said. "It'll be a pleasure."

She told me later that Captain Billy had come over. It was a good thing her parents were out that night. She was afraid to tell them anything about my problem. We were sure they'd never understand.

"Okay, missy, where is he?" he asked.

"Luke? I don't know and I don't care," she said. "He nearly hurt me. I never want to see him again."

"Come on, you can't fool Captain Billy! You've hidden him away. I know it. Just tell me and I'll go easy on him. He's a sick boy. He needs help."

"You're right about that. Believe me, if I knew where he was, I'd tell you. I think he belongs back in the hospital."

This went on and on. Finally, Captain Billy gave up.

Mariel came down that evening with some leftover chicken and rice and some apple juice.

"He'll be back," I said. "He won't give up this easily. He knows it's war now between us, and he wants to win."

It was a good thing I knew Captain Billy so well because a few days later when everyone was out of the house, I heard his footsteps.

I had been sleeping on the couch and almost cried out, "Who's there?"

Then I knew who it was. I don't know how he got into the house. He must have broken in. Now he was after me. I slipped behind the couch, held my breath, and prayed.

He was coming closer and closer. I could hear him. He was trying to be as quiet as he could, but his footsteps became louder as he got closer.

Captain Billy must have had a flashlight because I could see a beam coming nearer. He swung it around from the top of the dark basement to the floor.

He was almost at the couch now. I could hear him breathing. He moved the light up and down. He was almost on me, when I felt something brush against me and jump out at Billy.

"Argh! Get away, you beast!" he cried.

He turned away and ran up the steps. It was a rat. I had been saved by a rat. I hoped the rat wouldn't come near me again. But even a rat was better than being found by Captain Billy.

Chapter 17

Tea and Cake and Whiskey

Mariel's folks found the window Captain Billy had broken to get in. Since nothing was taken, they didn't call the police. They had the window fixed and put new locks on the windows and doors.

Mariel came down and gave me a copy of the new keys.

"Thanks," I said. "It's a big help to be able to go upstairs when everyone's gone for the day. I can even turn on the TV if I put it on low."

"Just be careful," said Mariel. "Our neighbors are home in the daytime. They could hear you."

"I'll be quiet," I said. "I don't want Captain Billy coming back."

"Captain Billy won't come snooping around here anymore, but that still doesn't help us," said Mariel. "We've got to find a way to deal with him."

"No deals," I said. "We've got to finish him off. If he finds me, there's no telling what he'll do to me."

"Maybe you could talk to your mother," she said.

"I don't know. I don't know if she still wants to marry him or what."

"How can your mother stand him?" she asked.

"Beats me. I can't believe she'll be fooled by him too long. Mom's really smart," I said. "She's just a little mixed up now. He's the first man she's gone out with since Dad died. But I am a little worried about her."

"I could go over there and see what's going on," Mariel said.

"I wish you would. The more I think about it, the more I think something strange is going on with her. It's not like her not to come to the hospital to see me."

"I'll go over tonight," she said. "I'll ask her if she's heard from you and tell her how sorry I am about you."

"Sounds good," I said. "Just watch out for Captain Billy."

Mariel told me about her visit later that night. It was past ten o'clock when she came down to the basement crying.

"What's wrong?" I asked. "Are you okay?"

"I'm fine," she said. "But I'm really afraid for your mother."

Then she told me her story.

At first, the visit had been like always. Mariel had gone over after dinner. She and Mom really liked each other, and they enjoyed the time they spent together.

Mom made some tea and put out some cake. Captain Billy was out, so she and Mariel were alone together.

When Mariel started to talk about me, though, she said Mom seemed scared.

"Do you think there's really something wrong with Luke?" she asked Mariel.

"I think he needs your help," said Mariel.

"I wish I could help him," she said, "but I'm not sure what to do now. I know Luke's a good boy. He's always been good."

Right after she said that, the door banged open.

"Who's always been good?" asked Captain Billy.

"No one," said Mom. "How about some tea and cake, Bill?"

"I don't want any tea," he said. "Tea is for old ladies. Where's the whiskey?"

"It's gone, Bill," she said. "Don't you remember? You finished it last night."

"Then why haven't you bought some more? How's a man to live without whiskey? I can't drink tea."

Mariel could see that Captain Billy was drunk. He was walking around the room, trying hard not to bump into the table and chairs.

"Come on, Bill," said Mom. "How about some coffee if you don't want tea?" She tried to put her arm around him.

"I said I want whiskey." He pushed her away so hard she banged into the wall.

"Mrs. Mason, are you all right?" cried Mariel.

"And what's she doing here?" asked Captain Billy. "I know she knows where that little rat of yours is hiding. I'll find him, and when I do, he'd better watch out!"

"I told you I don't know where Luke is, and if you don't stop this, I'm going to call the police," Mariel said.

Captain Billy smiled. "Just try it, missy," he said. "I'll have them on you and your boyfriend in no time flat. After all, he escaped from the hospital. No one said he could leave."

Mariel went over to try and help Mom up.

"Please, let me be," said Mom. "Please go home now. I'll be all right."

"But Mrs. Mason, I'm worried about you," said Mariel. "You can't stay here alone with him."

Captain Billy was opening all the closets and drawers looking for whiskey. He was throwing things on the floor as he searched.

"He never did this before," Mom said. "Maybe he'll give up and go out again if he wants a drink. I think he'll come home in the morning and tell me he's sorry."

"You can live with him like this?" asked Mariel. "You don't have to put up with it."

Mom just looked away. She started to cry.

"Please go home, Mariel. I'll call you."

"No, I'm not leaving until he does."

By this time, both of them were crying. Captain Billy took a look at them.

"Crying like babies," he said. "And not a drop to drink in this house. You certainly don't know how to take care of a man. I'll be on my way."

He slammed out of the door without looking back.

"He's gone," said Mariel. "Please, Mrs. Mason, pack a bag and come home with me."

"I can't," Mom said. "What would I tell your folks? They'd say it served me right for taking him in. That's what most people would think."

"What do you care what people think?" asked Mariel. "I want you to be safe. That's much more important."

"I'm sure Bill won't hurt me. I can't leave this apartment," said Mom. "If I did, I'd never get it back."

"Why don't you just tell Bill to leave?" asked Mariel.

"I'd like to," Mom said. "But he's bigger and stronger than I am. He might just laugh at me. I can't force him. I'd call the police but I'm afraid for Luke."

"So you're not going to marry Bill?" asked Mariel.

"All I want is to get him out of my life. Luke was right. He's no good. I made a big mistake."

"I'm sure Luke would be happy to hear that," said Mariel.

"Do you know where he is?" asked Mom. "The hospital said he tried to hurt you, and then he escaped."

"He didn't hurt me, Mrs. Mason. But that's all I'm going to tell you. Captain Billy mustn't know where Luke is."

"Don't worry," Mom said. "I don't tell him anything anymore."

"You know it was Bill's idea to put him in the hospital. Luke isn't crazy," said Mariel.

"I thought so," said Mom. "But I was afraid to do anything because of Bill. Just tell me, is Luke safe?"

"He's safe now. If Captain Billy gets a hold of him, he won't be."

"Then I'll have to get rid of Bill, won't I?"

"He's a dangerous man," said Mariel. She was afraid to tell Mom any more than that.

Mom thought for a moment. "Don't worry," she said. "This is thefirst time he's tried something like this. I can take care of myself."

Mariel had to leave her like that. She asked Mom again to go with her, but Mom wouldn't.

"Just tell Luke to take care of himself, and tell him I love him."

After she walked home, Mariel started crying again.

"I'm so worried about her," she said to me.

I couldn't talk for a minute, I was so angry and worried.

"I have to get out of here. I'm going to get Captain Billy," I said as I walked around the basement. "He can't treat her like that. I'll take care of him."

Mariel just watched me. I walked up and down, feeling angry and helpless. How could I get out when the hospital and the police were looking for me? All I had to do was show up for Captain Billy to get me locked up forever.

"You know, I just thought of something," Mariel said. "I think maybe Captain Billy was putting on a little show for me."

"What do you mean?"

"Your mother said he hadn't acted this way before. I know he still thinks I know where you are. I bet treating your mother badly is his way of getting at you. He figures you'll get mad enough to come after him."

"Maybe you're right. I certainly am mad enough to leave the basement and go get him," I said.

"That's just what he wants," said Mariel. "Then he can call the police and the hospital and have you picked up. That'll take care of you nicely."

"Captain Billy is no dummy," I said. "I was ready to rush out and start a fight with him."

"That won't help you or your mother."

"We have to get Mom out of there," I said. "Now I see why she didn't come to visit me in the hospital. She's afraid of him. I guess the best news I've heard is that she isn't going to marry him."

"Yes, but we have to think about how we can take care of Captain Billy. We can get your mother out of the house. Captain Billy has to sleep sometime. But she doesn't want to leave. She's afraid he'll trash the house when she's gone just because he's so mean."

"I've been thinking, and I might have an idea. After all, I don't want to stay in the basement for the rest of my life."

"That's good because I don't think I can keep sneaking you leftovers. My mom thinks I'm eating way too much," said Mariel. "She thinks it's weird."

"I'll probably need just a few more days. I need you to do two more things for me. Please go up to the hospital and find Dr. Ramirez. Ask him these questions that I've written down."

"Okay. What's the other thing?"

"I need some books. Here are the subjects."

"These are all about light and what it does," she said. "I have to see if we have any books on this subject."

"I need a plan of the Con Edison plant, if you can get it. And while you're at it, see if you can find out where the fuse box is in my mother's building," I said.

"I'll try. Can I ask you what your idea is?"

"I'd rather not say until I've thought about it and read a little," I said. "I don't want to get our hopes up if it's not possible. But let's just say I'm thinking about how to shine a little less light on the subject of Captain Billy, something he won't like at all."

PART

<u>3</u>

Chapter 18

Jack Comes Back

Mariel was right. No one came down to the basement. The weather was warm, and the heat wasn't on.

So I was able to turn on the lights without worrying that someone would see me. Mariel got me the books I needed. It took me three days to read the books. I looked at the plan of the Con Edison plant. Then I had to think about what I was going to do and how I was going to do it. My first idea, to make sure there was a city-wide blackout, wasn't possible. I saw it would be too hard to break into the Con Edison plant. I was in the middle of thinking about another idea one night, when Mariel ran down the steps into the basement.

"I've got lots of news," she said. "First, I saw Dr. Ramirez. I asked him your questions, and you were right."

"That's a load off my mind," I said.

"And guess who's back?" Mariel asked.

"I can't guess," I said. I was trying to find something in a book.

"It's Jack," she said. "Jack's back."

I put down the book. "He came back," I said. "Is he in trouble with the police about the fire?"

"That's the best part," she said. "He was able to show them that he wasn't near the store the night of the fire. He was at a movie. At the movie theater, they remembered Jack because he had told them the sound on the movie was bad and then helped them fix the projector."

"That's just like Jack. Where did you see him?" I asked. "That's the best part," Mariel said. "He was at your mother's house. I think she'll tell Captain Billy to get lost soon."

"That would be great," I said, "but I have to make sure Captain Billy stays lost. Captain Billy's not going to pick up and leave without doing something about me."

"Why do you think so? Don't you think he'd just rather sneak away? After all, there are plenty of other women out there," she said.

"I don't think he's that much in love with Mom. But don't forget that I know he set the fire at Jack's, and I know who he is and where he came from. Most important of all, I think I know how to send him back. He's never going to feel safe until he's gotten rid of me."

"How are you coming with your plan?" she asked.

"Slow but sure. I'm working it out."

"Don't take too long," she said. "I think things are going to happen pretty soon."

After that, Mariel told me what was going on with Jack and Mom. She tried to see Mom every day. Mariel knew I was worried about her.

"I think your mother's really getting to like Jack," Mariel said. "Captain Billy looked angry tonight when he saw Jack was there."

Another night she told me about Jack's plans to rebuild his shop.

"He's going to make a bigger window so he can put more furniture in it. He's going to make a wooden sign shaped like a table. He's got great plans," she said. "He asked me about you."

"What did he ask?"

"Oh, like when are you planning on coming back. How are you. That kind of thing," she said.

My need to see Mom and Jack was getting stronger and stronger. That's when I took my biggest chance.

"Mariel, tomorrow night I'm going to see Mom," I said. "Let her know. Make sure she gets rid of Captain Billy."

"Are you sure you want to do this?" she asked. "You've only been out of the hospital for a week and a half. Captain Billy is still looking for you."

"I have to take the chance," I said. I didn't tell her I was feeling trapped, but I guess she got the idea. I just had to get outside.

"Okay, I'll tell your mother," she said. "What about Jack? He seems to be over there all the time now."

131

"You can tell him, too, but don't tell him anything about the fire or about who Captain Billy really is," I said. "Even Mom and Jack wouldn't believe it. They'll think it's all part of the hospital thing."

"That's for sure. I wouldn't even know how to begin to explain it," she said.

The next night I waited until it was dark. Then I slipped out of the basement. Mariel met me on the corner, and we started walking. She had found an old sweatshirt with a hood for me. I pulled the hood up over my head.

"I don't think anybody saw us," she said.

"It doesn't matter anymore," I said. "The only one I'm hiding from is Captain Billy."

My building was only seven blocks away from hers, but by the time we got there my heart was beating as if I had run a five-mile race.

I slipped around the side of the building. Mariel went up to see if Captain Billy was there. It seemed forever until she came down and said, "All clear."

"I'll keep watch in case Captain Billy comes home sooner than we thought," she said.

"Okay," I said, "I won't be long."

"Take as long as you want," she said. "I'll sit on the stoop. I'll be fine."

Mom started crying when she saw me. "Luke! I missed you so," she sobbed. We hugged until she stopped crying.

"You look so thin and tired," she said.

"I haven't been eating that many full meals," I said, "mostly leftovers."

"Good to see you, son," said Jack. He threw an arm around me and gave me a quick hug, too.

"Luke, the hospital people were looking for you last week," Mom said. "Mariel told me you never hurt her. Why were they looking for you? What happened?"

"Captain Billy must have gotten them to look for me when I first escaped," I said. "I really haven't done anything wrong. Mariel talked to Dr. Ramirez. From what he said, they would have had to let me go pretty soon anyway. I hadn't gotten into any fights, and I had done everything they said. They would have had to get a court hearing to keep me. No one at the hospital ever wrote to get one. They only kept me longer to please Dr. Rogers. He doesn't seem to be very interested anymore. He's got some new cases he's working on. There's only one person who wants me back there now—Captain Billy."

"Bill told me you were very sick, and the doctors said you'd have to stay there for months," my mother said. "He told me they said I shouldn't visit. It would only upset you."

"He lied to you," I said.

My mother started to cry again. "I'm so sorry I ever let that man into my house."

"I think you should just tell him to go, Mary," said Jack.

133

"I'll tell him tonight," said Mom. "When he comes home, I'll tell him to pack up and leave."

"Make sure Jack is here with you," I said. I didn't want to say any more and scare Mom, but I didn't want her alone with Captain Billy.

"Don't worry," said Jack. "I'll be here." He reached over to hold Mom's hand. They smiled at each other.

"But what are you going to do now, Luke?" Mom asked. "Can't you come home?"

"I want to," I said, "but I have to take care of a few things first. Believe me, I'll be home as soon as I can. I can't wait to sleep in my own bed again."

"I don't understand. What do you have to do that's so important you can't come home?" Mom asked.

"Don't worry, Mom," I said. "I'll be home as soon as I can."

"When you come back, there'll be a job for you," Jack said. "I'm going to start my business again. I'd like your help."

"Of course," I said. We didn't say any more. We understood each other, Jack and I.

I left a half hour later, feeling good about seeing Mom and Jack. They seemed to have found each other. It was great not to worry about Mom anymore. I knew Jack would be able to take care of her.

I wasn't worried about the hospital anymore. All I had to do now was get rid of Captain Billy. That would be the hardest thing of all to do.

I went downstairs and looked for Mariel. I didn't see her. Maybe she had gotten tired of waiting, although that wasn't like her.

Just then I heard her cry. "Luke!" Then the noise stopped as if someone had put his hand over her mouth. I knew who that someone was.

"Okay, Captain, let her go," I said. "You're looking for me, not her."

"That's right," said Captain Billy. He had his arm around Mariel's neck and he was making her walk with him.

"This is between you and me," I said. I tried to get Mariel away from him, but Captain Billy was strong. He hung on to her.

Mariel bit Captain Billy. "Aargh!" He sank to his knees from the pain. I kicked him in the stomach.

"Go on! Get help!" I yelled to Mariel. She ran back to the apartment. I knew she would get Jack. I thought I would have time to wait, but Captain Billy pulled out a knife.

"That hurt, boy," he gasped. "I was going to be easy on you, but forget it. All bets are off now."

He started to get to his feet. I didn't wait to see if Jack was coming. I ran as fast as I could.

I thought I was fast, but I could hear Captain Billy behind me. I ran faster. Even so, he was starting to catch up to me.

Then I saw the subway station ahead of me. Without stopping, I raced down the steps. I could hear a train coming into the station. No time to stop for a token. I jumped the turnstile and ran down the platform.

The doors opened, and I raced into the car. If luck was with me, we would pull out of the station before Captain Billy could get on. I looked out the window. I saw Captain Billy coming down the platform. He didn't know which way I had gone. He was looking in the cars. The bell rang. The doors started to close. Captain Billy was still six cars away. I had made it.

Then the doors opened again.

"There's a train up ahead. We'll be moving soon," the conductor said over the loudspeaker.

I didn't move. My only hope was that somehow, some way, Captain Billy wouldn't see me.

I could feel him coming closer. I closed my eyes and prayed for the train to move. The bell rang again, and the doors closed. I opened my eyes. Captain Billy wasn't in the car. Everything would be all right. I was okay. I had escaped.

Then I looked down the train, through the glass door and saw Captain Billy staring at me from the next car.

Chapter 19

In the Dark

I wasn't ready. That's the first thing I thought as I looked at Captain Billy. I had the beginnings of a plan, but I thought I would have a lot more time to work it out. Captain Billy had surprised me by acting sooner than I thought he would.

The only thing that was on my side was that it was dark. I had noticed that Captain Billy was careful to stay in the light at night. He never took long walks in the dark. He always stayed inside near the light—the brighter the better. He even kept the light on in the living room all night. He had given Mom extra money for the electric bill.

I was about to take Captain Billy for a walk on the dark side. It was my only chance. But first, I had to get out of the subway station without Captain Billy catching me.

I was in luck. A group of high school kids got on the train. They were dressed the way I was—in jeans and sweatshirts. They talked about getting off at Jay Street. If I could just stay with them, I'd be okay.

They started talking about basketball. Great. I had a way in.

It turned out they knew the guys I played basketball with at the Y. Soon we were talking about the Knicks and their chances this year. I didn't get so lost in the talk that I didn't keep an eye out for Captain Billy. So far he had kept his distance. As soon as he saw me with the guys, he stayed in his own car. But I knew he'd try to get me as soon as I was alone.

The train rushed through Brooklyn. Fourth Avenue. Smith and Ninth Streets. Carroll Street. Bergen Street. Soon we were downtown. I walked out of the station with the guys. Captain Billy followed behind.

"We're going out for pizza," one of them said. "You want to come along, Luke?"

I thought about asking them to help me, but that wouldn't fix Captain Billy for good. And that's what I wanted to do.

"Thanks but no thanks," I said. "Another time. I've got to meet some people."

Captain Billy watched as they walked away. Then he came up to me, but I was ready for him. I ducked into a movie theater—the closest and darkest place I knew. It would give me a little time to plan and make him want to get me even more. Maybe he would be so angry he'd make a mistake or two. I could use that.

I sat in the dark theater for three hours until the next show was half over. It was almost eleven. Then I walked into the lobby and looked out at the street.

Captain Billy was waiting outside. The street lights were dim. It had been hot lately, and Con Edison was trying to save the power. They had turned the power down all over town.

I had hoped he'd have to wait out in the dark. He couldn't take the chance to go inside. He couldn't wait in a restaurant or a bar that had light, or he might miss me when I came out.

After three hours in the dim light, he looked a little pale around the edges.

Good! Now to make it look even darker for him. I went back inside and waited for the movie to be over. There was a big crowd for the show and when it was over, I walked out with them.

It took Captain Billy a while to spot me. When he did, he tried to make his way through all the people. But he was going the wrong way, against the crowd. I made good time as I walked the few blocks to the next darkest place I knew, the Brooklyn Bridge.

Overhead, I could hear the hum of the cars as they crossed the bridge. There were lights on top of the bridge. But where I was going—under the bridge—there was little light at all. I had been on a tour one day and been taken into the wine vaults under the bridge. They were some of the darkest places I had ever been. I was willing to play hide-and-seek there with Captain Billy all night long.

I made sure Billy saw me as I slipped into the vaults. I wasn't sure if he'd follow. He could give up and try to get me another day. On the other hand, he knew I'd have to come out some time. I couldn't stay there all night.

I waited and waited. Would he try it? Finally, I heard footsteps on the brick floor. I had been wearing sneakers, so I hadn't made a sound. Now I could hear him walking towards me. I moved deeper into the darkness.

"Who's there?" I heard a strange voice.

The next thing I knew a light was shining in my eyes.

"Who are you and what are you doing here?" It was the night watchman. I had forgotten that somebody took care of this part of the bridge to make sure no one broke in.

"I thought I saw that thief come in here." I knew that voice. It was Captain Billy's.

"What did he take from you?" the night watchman asked.

"My wallet," said Captain Billy.

"Wait a minute," I said. "I didn't take anything. You can look through my pockets. I don't have anything on me."

"He must have gotten rid of it when he saw we were about to catch him," said Captain Billy.

"No way," I said. "This man is out to get me. He has a knife. He's trying to kill me."

The night watchman looked at both of us.

"Why would you believe a young hoodlum like him?" asked Captain Billy.

"Never mind," I said. "Let's get the police in here."

"I think that's a good idea," said the night watchman. "You two stay here while I call the police."

"No need for that," said Captain Billy. "But if you really want to call them, the boy and I will wait here."

The night watchman walked away to the front of the vault. Billy watched him go and then pulled out his knife.

"What a shame I'm going to have to kill you, Luke," he said. "You tried to kill me, and I had to take care of myself. At least, that's the story I'll tell the police."

"You're not going to get me, you murderer," I said.

We circled each other slowly. Captain Billy had the knife, but I was faster on my feet. All of a sudden, he moved in and tried to cut my arm. But I jumped back. The moves I'd learned playing basketball paid off.

I could hear the night watchman talking. I was afraid to get into a close fight with Captain Billy because he was bigger and heavier, plus he had the knife. It was hard to move on the uneven brick floor of the vault. If I could just keep him away from me a few minutes more until the night watchman came back, I'd be okay.

But I was getting awfully tired of letting Captain Billy get the first shots in all the time. I could feel myself getting more and more angry.

I tried to grab his arm, the one with the knife. Billy moved in closer and tried to bend my arm behind me. I punched him in the stomach, and moved away. He seemed to be moving more and more slowly. He kept looking around.

"What's the matter, Captain?" I asked. "Afraid of the dark? Or should I say the Underdark?"

"I won't go back there," he said. "I'll do anything I can to make sure of that. But if by any chance I do, you're going with me."

"No way," I said. "You'll never get me." I moved away from his knife arm.

"All I need is an hour in the light," he said. "That'll do it. But first I'm going to get rid of you."

He moved towards me with the knife. I moved back, fell over a loose brick, and went flying.

I landed on the cold floor with Captain Billy over me, the knife in his hand, ready to kill me.

"What's going on here?" the night watchman asked. He flashed his light over us. Then he saw the knife in Billy's hand.

"Put that knife away!" he yelled.

Billy ran toward him, and pushed him to one side. The night watchman fell. Billy ran out into the night.

"Are you all right?" I asked. I stopped to help the night watchman up.

"I'm okay. But did I see right? Did that guy have a knife?"

"Yeah. I told you he was after me," I said.

"The police will take care of him," the night watchman said. "They'll be here any minute."

"I can't wait," I said. "If I wait for them, I'll never take care of Captain Billy."

I ran out of the vault and headed for the nearest subway. I knew now what I had to do. I was careful not to go near any bright lights. I was sure Billy would be waiting there—getting his strength back to finish me off. I had to take care of him first. What I had to do wasn't safe, wasn't smart, and a lot of people would say it wasn't good. I had thought and thought about ways to get rid of Billy and had come up with two plans. The first plan hadn't worked. Now it was time to try the second one.

I ran along the dark waterfront. I could hear the ferry honking in the distance and the slap of the waves against the pier. The only light came from across the river—the tall buildings of the New York skyline, lit up and shining against the blackened sky and a string of lights from the South Street pier.

Couples were sitting quietly on benches enjoying the view. It was a beautiful sight, but I couldn't stop to enjoy it. My sides hurt from running, and my chest felt as if it were on fire when I finally got to where I needed to go—the subway station.

Captain Billy was out there somewhere, following me and waiting. I could only hope I was right and that he was close behind me. But not too close.

Chapter 20

A Chance in the Dark

The train rushed into the station, blowing the old newspapers and candy wrappers up in the air. As it screeched to a stop, I looked back and saw Captain Billy slip into the station behind me.

It was late, and only four people stood between me and Captain Billy. Those four people—a woman who looked as if she had been working late, a young guy and his girlfriend, and a transit cop—were enough to make sure Captain Billy wouldn't attack me on the train.

Now I had to pray that those people wouldn't get off before I did. Otherwise, Captain Billy would feel free to kill me. I had to travel only five stops.

I sat close to the door. Captain Billy sat across from me, watching my every move.

He jumped when the woman walked past me and left at the first stop. The guy and his girl were too busy looking at each other to notice, but the cop kept his eye on us.

Four more stops. Three more stops. The girl and the guy got out. I shut my eyes and prayed. Please, please don't let the cop leave before I do.

The stop before mine was coming up. I've noticed that sometimes people move a little before they get up to go. The cop made some of those little moves.

My heart started racing. The cop was getting up. Captain Billy started smiling. The train doors opened. The cop got out.

Captain Billy and I were alone on the train together. The bell rang. I could see Captain Billy start to reach into his pocket for his knife. He kept his eyes on me the whole time. I got ready to run. And then, two big guys walked into our car and sat down.

I could breathe again. I smiled.

"Don't worry. I'll get you yet," said Captain Billy.

"What's that?" asked one of the guys. "Are you talking to me?"

"No," said Billy. "Just talking to myself. It's that time of night."

"I don't believe you," said the guy. "I think you were talking to me."

"Aw, Joe, leave him alone," said his friend. "You're always looking for a fight."

"No old, beat-up guy's gonna talk to me that way," said Joe.

"Look, I said I wasn't talking to you," said Billy loudly.

"What do you think?" Joe asked me. "Do you think he was talking to me?"

"Seemed like it to me," I said. It was hard to keep from laughing. Captain Billy's big mouth had finally gotten him into trouble.

"I think he needs a lesson," Joe said. "Don't you?"

The train was coming to a stop.

"Sure do," I said. "Well, I've got to be going. Goodnight, all."

I ran out of the car. Billy tried to follow, but I saw Joe stop him. The doors closed and the train pulled out of the station. I couldn't believe my luck.

Now if my luck would only hold out until I reached a telephone, I'd be all set. I walked down the street looking for a working phone. If you have ever tried to find one in Brooklyn, you'd know it isn't easy.

Sometimes they're broken, and no one fixes them. Sometimes you think they're working, and you spend all your money, and your call never goes through. And you don't get your money back.

The first one I tried was broken. So was the second. It looked as if my luck had turned. Then I found one I thought worked. I only had two quarters on me. I put the first quarter in. I got a dial tone. I rang the number. No one answered. I never thought she wouldn't be home. It was one A.M. She had to be home.

I kept on ringing. No answer. Maybe she was asleep. I hung up. I heard footsteps coming. Was it Captain Billy?

I hid in a doorway. The footsteps came closer and closer. They sounded like a man's, but I couldn't be sure. Then I heard a strange breathing sound. Something was sniffing around.

I couldn't stand it. I stepped out of the doorway. It was a man walking his dog.

"Ah!" he yelled. I had surprised him by coming out of the doorway so fast.

He turned and started running. The dog ran after him, barking.

"It's okay," I yelled. "I won't hurt you."

He didn't stop. He just kept on running.

I went back to the phones. I walked down a block and tried a new one. This one worked and I rang the same number again. But this time Mariel answered. I must have dialed the wrong number before.

"Did I wake you?" I asked.

"No. I was worried about you," she said. "I couldn't sleep until I heard from you. Where did you go? Jack and I looked for you."

I said, "I don't have time to talk now. Here's what I need you to do. You have to go out now and . . ."

I told her what to do. She was one in a million. She didn't waste any time. She just told me she'd do it.

I hung up and walked the six blocks to Mom's house. It was hard to call it my own now. It felt as if I had been away for years.

I walked up the steps and rang the bell.

"Who's there?" I heard Mom call.

"It's me, Luke."

"Give me a minute."

She was in her robe and slippers when she opened the door. Poor Mom. She looked so tired.

"Luke!" She hugged and kissed me. "Let's go inside."

"I'll close the door," I said, but I made sure not to lock it. I looked around. She had turned on all the lights. It was very bright inside.

"Are you home for good?" she asked.

"I hope so. Is Captain Billy in?"

"He left a few days ago," she said. "I told him I couldn't have him stay here anymore. I made him give back his key. Luke, I have wonderful news."

"What's that, Mom?"

"Jack and I are going to get married."

"That's great," I said. "Jack is a great guy. I know you'll be happy with him."

"Yes, he's a lot like your father. No one will ever take your father's place, but Jack is a good man. I realized that Bill was not what I wanted at all. You were right about him, Luke."

"I'm glad," I said. I walked around and pulled down the shades on the windows. Then, I tried to relax, but I couldn't. I kept looking for Captain Billy. I was sure he'd come soon.

"What's the matter, Luke?" Mom asked. "You look as if you're worried about something."

The door burst open.

"He's got plenty to worry about." Captain Billy raced into the room. His shirt was torn. His nose was bleeding. His face had black and blue marks. His hair was all messed up.

"Did you have a little trouble, Captain?" I asked.

"I'll show you trouble. I told you I'd get you," he said.

"Please, Bill, go home and leave us alone. It's not Luke's fault I'm not going to marry you," said Mom.

"It's not only that, Mary," said Captain Billy. "After all, you're not the only woman around. But your son knows too much. He could make sure I go back to the Underdark."

"The what?" asked Mom.

"Never mind," he said. He pulled out his knife and started walking towards me.

Mom saw the knife and stepped between me and Captain Billy. He shoved her so hard she hit her head against the wall and fell to the floor.

"Mom! Are you okay?" I yelled.

"She'll be all right," Captain Billy said. "I didn't push her that hard. I guess I don't know my own strength."

"Yeah, you're a real hero when it comes to fighting with women," I said. "I'll be happy to fight with you. Just let me move Mom into the other room."

"Nothing doing," he said. "You're planning one of your tricks. I can tell."

"At least let me put her on the sofa," I said.

"I guess she should be lying down when she finds out her son is dead," said Captain Billy.

"You put things so well, Captain," I said.

I picked Mom up and put her down on the sofa.

"You know, I think you're right," he said. "I think she should be out of the way. What if she tries to help you? Put her in her room."

I picked Mom up again and took her to her room.

"And lock the door," said Captain Billy. "I don't want her coming to and getting out. Now give me the key."

Captain Billy moved in quickly with the knife and took the key away. Then he cut my arm and I jumped away.

It was just a small cut, but I backed away from him carefully. There wasn't much room to turn. I kept bumping into chairs and tables. The good thing was that Captain Billy couldn't get near me either. There was too much stuff in the way.

I looked at my watch.

"Going someplace?" asked Captain Billy.

"No, but you are . . . right about now," I said, as the lights in the apartment went dark. It was so dark I could hardly see in front of me.

"What's going on?" shouted Billy. "Where are you? Put some lights on!"

"What's going on, Captain, is what's called a 'blackout,'" I said.

"You planned this," he said. I tried to move away from his voice, but there wasn't anyplace to go.

"You're right about that. I called my girlfriend and asked her to take out the fuses. She went down to the basement and made sure they're all gone. Now you're stuck," I said. I didn't tell him I didn't know what to do next or whether I would be able to win any kind of fight against him.

"No I'm not," he said. "I'm getting out of here. As soon as it's light again, I'll take care of you."

"You don't understand, Captain," I said. "I've locked the door. You're stuck here until someone puts the fuses back in. And since it's one A.M. and everyone's asleep, I think we've got plenty of time to make sure you go back to the Underdark. Even if someone does wake up, I don't think they're going to be turning on any lights."

"Give me that front door key," he growled. He tried to rush towards me, but I was ready for him. I moved behind a chair.

"Ow!" he yelled.

"Hurt yourself, Captain? You'd better be careful in here. It's dark," I said.

I tried to sound as brave as I could, but I was really worried. I was trapped alone with this killer. He had a knife. I had nothing. I could only move away from him for so long. Sooner or later, he was going to get near me. I was only afraid he would finish me off before he got too weak from the darkness.

"Just keep talking, boy. I'll find you," he said. I realized he was using the sound of my voice to figure out where I was.

I kept as quiet as I could. I was wearing sneakers, so I could move without making a sound. Captain Billy was wearing boots. I could hear them thump softly as he moved closer.

Backing away from the noise, I felt the arm of a chair. It must have been the one my mother sat in most nights. I tried to remember what it looked like. It was big and round. Was it large enough to hide behind?

It's funny how you see things every day, but when it's important you can't remember what they look like.

I moved around the chair. Then I remembered the big sofa. I could slide under it, and Captain Billy would never find me. It was right next to the chair. I felt my way past the chair to the big arm of the sofa. I got down on the floor very, very quietly. I started to creep along the floor, ready to slide under the sofa.

"Luke! Luke! What's going on there? Where are you?"

I was afraid to answer her. I had found the perfect hiding place. If I called to her, Captain Billy might be able to tell where I was.

"Luke! Please answer me. I'm afraid. What's happened? Are you all right?" Mom kept calling.

Then she started banging on the door. "Help! Help!"

I couldn't stand it any longer.

"I'm okay, Mom," I called. "Don't worry. It's all right."

Then I felt someone grab my foot.

"Gotcha!" said Captain Billy.

Chapter 21

Under the Dark

I was halfway under the sofa and in a bad spot. There wasn't much I could do. I let Captain Billy pull me out. Then I jumped up and stepped on his hand as hard as I could.

"Ow!" he cried. I could hear him hop up and down from the pain. Then there was a clunk. He dropped something. I hoped it was the knife. I couldn't know for sure that he didn't have it any more. I had to take the chance. Captain Billy was bigger and stronger than I was, but I was going to have to fight him up close if I ever wanted to get out of there alive.

I moved in. All my basketball moves came back to me. But this time I wasn't looking to make a basket, I was trying to get rid of a man.

Oof! I bumped into something. I think it was the table. Now it was my turn to bite my lip from the pain. Neither one of us wanted to make any noise and give away where we were. But we both knew that it was the end for one of us. There was no escape.

Meanwhile, Mom kept banging on the door. I tried to get near it to whisper to her. I didn't make it. I ran into Captain Billy.

He punched me in the nose. I could feel the blood dripping down my face. Now I was not only afraid, I was mad.

I grabbed him and got in a few punches. Then he caught my head in a hammerlock. I kept punching him on his back, but he wouldn't let go.

Then I tried kicking him. But I couldn't get any strength.

"I've got you now," he said, "and if I can't get out of here and back to the light, I'm going to do what I said and take you with me to the Underdark."

I nearly passed out when I thought about it. Not only would I be going with Captain Billy, but John Cross, the shadow I had brought out and locked in the closet, would probably be waiting for me.

I had to get free. Captain Billy seemed to feel none of my punches or kicks. He was choking the life out of me.

As he was choking me, I thought I could hear the men in the Underdark yelling.

"Let us out," they called. "Give us light."

It sounded like thousands of them were calling me from the dark. I felt the pull of the darkness. I was getting weaker and weaker. I almost didn't mind slipping into the dark and falling into the waiting crowd of those searching for the light.

"Luke! Luke! Help me get out of here."

It was my mother's voice that brought me back to my senses.

I remembered what John Cross had said about the Underdark.

"It's terrible! Don't send me back there, please," he had cried when I had locked him in the closet.

I started fighting Captain Billy again. I did everything I could to get out of his hold. He seemed to be getting weaker, but he was still pretty strong. So I bit him as hard as I could on his arm.

"Argh! You little rat. You bit me!"

He dropped his hold, and I was able to slide out and away. I had to remember my plan. Keep Captain Billy in the dark as long as I could. John Cross had said that they all needed at least ten hours of light.

What I had learned from the books I read was that all growing things need light. If people didn't have light for a long time, it did strange things to them. Captain Billy needed light more than most.

All I had to do was stay in the dark room as long as I could and make sure Captain Billy didn't find any light. I would be all right, but he wouldn't. Sooner or later, he would catch on and try to get out.

"Got to get out of here," I heard him say. "Got to get to the window." I heard him moving slowly towards the wall.

It was going to be sooner. I'd have to make sure he didn't get there. Before I'd been trying to get away from him, now I was trying to find Captain Billy. I was as blind as he was in the dark. But I knew I would never get such a chance at him again.

I tried to move closer to where I thought the window was. I felt along the walls. My hand slipped and then I felt glass. I was at the window. Now I had to be sure Billy wouldn't push me through the glass to try and get to some light.

"The light! Light!" I heard Captain Billy talking to himself. He sounded as if he was getting weaker and weaker. His voice came closer and closer.

I rolled myself into a ball on the window seat. I could hear him breathing now, he was that close.

Then as soon as I felt him in front of me, I kicked out at him. I could hear the thump as he fell.

I had kicked him hard, but not hard enough to really hurt him, I thought. But I didn't hear Captain Billy get to his feet right away. Instead, I heard him crawling on the floor.

I slipped away from the window seat. I didn't want him to find me there and push me through it. I moved away, keeping my back to the wall. As I moved quietly away, I could hear my mother crying in the bedroom.

"Luke! Help! Someone tell me what's going on out there!"

Captain Billy couldn't keep his mouth shut.

"I'll tell you what's going on. I'm going to kill your son as soon as I get my hands on him. I'm going to finish that little rat off once and for all. And if I don't get him, I'm taking him with me. If I go back to the Underdark, the two of you had better watch out. I'll find some way of getting back and making sure I get both of you."

"No! Luke!" my mother started screaming. "Help! Police! Help!"

He was closer than I had thought. He got me by the neck again. But this time, he was much weaker than before.

"I think you're running out of steam, Captain," I managed to say before he got his hands around my neck.

"We'll see about that!"

Again I started to feel as if I was going to pass out.

"Say good-bye to your mother, boy. This is the end of you," he said.

I knew I had to keep my head. I couldn't let Captain Billy get the better of me now—not when he seemed to be getting weaker and weaker, not when I was so close to getting rid of him. He moved forward, and I banged against a table. His hands were still around my neck, choking the life out of me.

I grabbed the table and felt something on it that was big and heavy.

At first, I couldn't lift it. It seemed to be stuck.

Captain Billy was getting tired. I could feel it. I pulled the thing as hard as I could. Finally, I held it. I lifted it up and hit Captain Billy on the head.

"Ow!"

I had hit him but not hard enough to make him let go. I struck him again. I could feel him sag against me. I hit him one more time.

Then I heard him fall to the floor.

I waited for a few minutes to see if it was a trick. But Captain Billy seemed to be out cold.

"Luke! Are you there?" Mom called.

"It's okay, Mom. I'm all right. Where do you keep the flashlight?"

"In the table by the big chair," she answered.

It took me a while to feel around the room until I got to the big chair. I felt all over the table until I found the flashlight in it.

It seemed like ages until I turned it on.

Billy was lying on the floor. He was still alive and breathing, but he had a large bump on his head. A large glass vase lay next to him.

I looked at him. I didn't want to touch him but I had to get the key to let Mom out of the bedroom. I felt in his pockets and finally got the key.

Then I let Mom out. It took a while before she stopped crying.

"I was so afraid," she cried. "I couldn't do anything. I couldn't even get to the phone. What went on here?"

"Captain Billy tried to kill me," I said. I still

had trouble saying it.

"Why didn't you call the police?" Mom asked. "Someone could have helped you, even if I couldn't."

"It wouldn't have done any good. The police never would have believed me. Look what happened at the hospital. The doctors all believed Captain Billy. This was something I had to do myself," I said. That was what had scared me the most. I couldn't ask anyone else to help me. I was the only one who could deal with Captain Billy.

And speaking of taking care of him, I still had to figure out what to do with him.

"Do you have any heavy string or rope?" I asked.

"In the kitchen," Mom said. "What are you going to do?"

"Now that Captain Billy's out cold, I'm going to go down to the basement and tell Mariel to put the fuses back in. Then I'm going to tie Billy up until I can figure out what to do with him," I said.

"I'll help you," she said.

"All right. But don't get too close to Captain Billy. I think he's still dangerous even though he's a lot weaker."

Mariel jumped when she heard us come into the basement.

"Luke, I was so scared. It was hard to sit here like you told me. I wanted to help you."

"You did. The lights went out just when I

wanted them to," I said.

We went back up to Mom's and turned on the lights. We got the string and then we went into the living room. As I walked in, I saw the knife on the floor and picked it up. Captain Billy still lay where I had left him, but his eyes were open now.

"How are you feeling, Captain?" I asked. I held the knife tightly. He didn't look at me. He didn't seem to hear me. He was staring into space at something terrible from the look on his face.

"Captain Billy, can you hear me?" I asked.

"No," he screamed. "I can see it. I can't go. Please, please don't let me go. I can't stand it. I'm slipping away. The darkness . . . the darkness . . . the darkness . . ."

He reached his hand out. I was afraid to take it. Knowing Captain Billy, it might still be a trick. I didn't want to get anywhere near him. Mariel stayed behind me. I think she felt the same way.

Mom was more tenderhearted.

"Oh, Bill, don't worry. We'll make sure you get some help," she said. "We'll call a doctor. You'll be okay." She went to take his hand.

Then I realized what was happening.

"Mom, don't touch him," I screamed. I pushed her aside.

"It's all right, Luke," she said. "He won't hurt us now." She moved forward to take his hand again. He was still holding it out to her.

"Please, Mary," he said.

I stepped in front of her.

"Forget it, Captain," I said. "She's not going with you. You're going alone."

"Too smart for your own good," Captain Billy said. Then, all of a sudden, his face relaxed and he stopped breathing. Without any life in him, he looked more like a gray shadow than a man lying on the floor.

"Oh, no, he's dead," cried my mother. "What are we going to do now?"

"I'll call the police," I said. "He was going to kill me. I was right to defend myself."

"I'll call my uncle after you call the police," said Mariel. "He'll make sure nothing bad happens to you."

"But what did he die of?" Mom asked. "He couldn't have died from your hitting him. He had his eyes open. He talked to us."

"I didn't hit him that hard," I said.

"Maybe he had a heart attack," Mom said. "We won't find out until we call the police."

I thought Mom looked as if she was in shock. Mariel must have thought so, too.

"I'll make us some tea," she said. "I think we all need something for the shock."

Mom went with Mariel to the kitchen to make the tea while I went to call the police.

I went to the phone. I dialed 911. I looked over at the body. Captain Billy looked small to me, much smaller than he had looked when he was alive.

An operator came on the line, and I turned

back to the phone.

"Hello, I'd like to report . . . ."

Then the strangest thing of all happened. I looked over at Captain Billy's body again. One minute it was there, a small gray shadow, and the next it wasn't. I put down the phone.

"Hello . . . hello . . ." I could hear the operator talking. I looked all around. Only the vase was left where Captain Billy had been lying. Then I walked back to the phone and hung it up.

Mom and Mariel came into the room with the tea. Mom had her head turned away from the spot where Captain Billy had been lying.

"I can't bear to look at him," she said.

"You won't have to," I said. "He's gone."

"You mean he didn't die?" Mom asked. "I can't believe it. He looked dead to me. How did he get out of the house? I never heard him go."

"He didn't leave the usual way," I said. "But we don't have to worry about him anymore."

Mariel looked at me. I think she guessed what had happened.

"It's the Underdark, isn't it?" she asked.

"Luke, you didn't do anything you shouldn't have, did you?" Mom asked. "You didn't hide the body, did you? We really have to tell the police about this."

"Mom, let me tell you a story," I said. "You're going to find this hard to believe but . . . ."

Chapter 22

Into the Light

It took a long time to tell Mom the story and even longer for her to believe me. She kept shaking her head and looking at me strangely. I was lucky that Mariel knew the true story, although even she didn't know everything.

"You're making this up," Mom kept saying. "This couldn't be true."

"It's true, Mom," I said. "Please believe me. Didn't you think there was anything strange about Captain Billy?"

"I did think he was out of touch," Mom said. "He didn't know a lot about what was going on in the world. But I thought it was because he had been out to sea so much that he didn't know what was going on. He seemed as if he was a nice old-fashioned gentleman."

"But what about that night I came over?" Mariel asked. "He acted so bad. I was really afraid."

"That was the first time he had shown that side of himself to me," Mom said. "Most of the time he was very nice. But what do you think happened to him? Where could the body have gone?"

"I think the Underdark took him back," I said. "I should have seen it. When he first came out, he looked like a shadow. And after he stopped breathing, he started looking like a shadow again. I think he ran out of the light he needed, and the pull of the Underdark was too strong."

"What an awful way to die," Mom said.

"I don't think he's really dead. He's alive in the Underdark. He just hasn't come to light," I said.

"Yuck! It gives me the creeps to think of him somewhere around," said Mariel. "I never want to see him again."

"I think I know how to make sure he doesn't," I said. "I read the books about light that you got me. I couldn't find anything to tell me why Captain Billy came through me into the light. But I did figure something out. The speed of the train and the light waves happened to meet at the same time."

"Were you just standing in the wrong place?" Mariel asked.

"Something like that. John Cross told me they all tried to catch the light waves and ride them into our world. I think the Captain just got stuck when he hit me," I told her.

"So it was just bad luck," Mom said.

"Yes, I never want to go through that again," I answered.

"You know, he tried to take you with him, Mom."

"When was that?" she asked.

"When he reached out for you at the end," I said. "Remember he tried to take your hand?"

"I thought he just wanted me to help him," she said.

"Oh, no, Captain Billy thought he could pull you into the Underdark with him. That way he would have gotten back at me."

"So that's why he said you were too smart for your own good," she said.

"Do you think there are people from the Underdark around now?" Mariel asked.

"I don't know. But from what John Cross told me, I think it's very hard for them to get into this world. I think what happened to us was just bad luck."

We talked some more about it. I think we were all afraid that Captain Billy might come back.

Mom came with me when I walked Mariel home. I think she was afraid to be alone, and I thought it was a good idea if we stayed together. But she gave us a few minutes alone together, long enough for me to thank Mariel for everything.

"I couldn't have gotten rid of Captain Billy without you," I said.

"I was just glad I could help you. But it was just awful waiting in that dark basement, not knowing what was going on," she said.

"I had to do it that way. If there were other people around, I was afraid he might hurt them or try to take them with him the way he tried with Mom," I said. "I had to do it alone."

When Mom and I got back home, we went to bed right away. I've never been so tired in my life. Both of us thought we would have nightmares, but strangely enough we both slept well. It felt good to sleep in my own bed again.

The next morning I got up early. Mom heard me and called, "Where are you going, Luke?"

"There's one more person I have to talk to," I said. "I'll be back in an hour or so."

Of course she knew the person I meant. I had to talk to Jack. I realized that when he had asked me to work with him again I had never told him I was the reason his shop had burned down. I had to tell him and see if he still wanted me to work with him.

He was working on his shop sign when I walked in.

"Luke, I'm glad to see you," he said. He came forward and gave me a hug and a slap on the back.

It made it even harder for me to tell him the story, but I did. I didn't want him to be the only one of us four who didn't know. And I felt bad that because of me Captain Billy had burned his shop down.

Jack listened. He didn't say a word until I had finished.

"It's hard to believe," he said.

"It's true," I said. "You can ask Mom or Mariel. Both of them saw Captain Billy's body."

"I don't have to ask. I believe you. I trust you. That's why I wanted to work with you," he said.

"Jack, I feel awful that your shop was burned down because of me," I said.

"I'm not so sure that's true," he said.

"Captain Billy did burn your shop down," I said. "I'm sure of that."

"That part's true," he said. "But I think Bill did it because he wanted me to stay away from your mother. I don't think it was really about you. And for a while, he got his wish. I was too busy feeling sorry for myself. Luckily, I finally came to my senses."

"Is the job still open?" I asked.

"I was hoping you'd come by," he said. "I'd like it to be more than just a job."

Then he showed me the sign he had been working on. Mariel was right. It was in the shape of a table. But there was more. It read: "Conley and Mason."

So I started working with Jack. It was nothing like the hospital. I was doing something I loved, working with a man who became a second father to me.

Jack and Mom got married a few months later. Everybody was happy about that. Jack wants me to take a business class at the local college, and I'm going to do it. I can't say I'm looking forward to going back to school, but maybe it will mean something to me this time since I'll learn something I can use.

I am happy to say I've never seen Dr. Rogers or any of the other doctors from the hospital since. If I ever get sick, I wouldn't go back there.

Mariel and I have started making plans for the future. She wants to go back to school, and I want to make sure that the shop is the place I want to be. So we're not rushing into anything yet. But we know we'll be together. It's just a matter of time.

I try to forget what happened with Captain Billy as much as I can. I think I was really lucky that no one was hurt and that the Underdark pulled him back. But sometimes when it's very bright out and I'm in the light too long, I feel strange, as if Captain Billy is out there just waiting for me. I can't help looking at the light, but I never, ever ride in the first car of the subway anymore. And I never will.